# Yours, Anonymous

Peter David Orr

Beachfront
PRESS

# BEACHFRONT PRESS

THIRD EDITION, December 2017



Orr, Peter David

Yours, Anonymous/ Peter David Orr

ISBN 978-098277647-6

# Prologue

Have you ever heard about something that just doesn't seem to add up? The death of Ashley White is that way for me. I can't seem to let it go, despite the fact that Ashley and I were never even friends. He was a grade ahead of me in High School and we only had one class together.

There was something about what I witnessed in this matter that has gripped me and won't let go. I feel like an injustice has been done, and it has driven me to do things I never thought possible. Believe me, I would rather not be known in school as "the girl obsessed with Ashley's death." I certainly don't enjoy the incessant whispering going on behind my back every day at Franklin. I get it. To many of you, I'm just "that crazy detective chick." So be it. If you read this and remain unmoved by what I've revealed through these interviews, please move on with your life and stay clear of me and my friends. Seriously.

For the rest of you: if you can relate to wanting to get at the truth, then please read this short book and join me in a quest for justice. At the very least, this sort of thing should never happen again at any school.

Initially, I refrained from editorializing because I hoped these interviews would speak for themselves, but as time went on, my inner prosecutor won out. For this reason the reader will find an overview of the events which led to Ashley White's death, as well as my commentaries following many of the interviews. I make no apologies if the overview comes across like an opening statement in a criminal trial, or for expressing strong opinions.

Each interview transcript was verified for authenticity and accuracy by the teacher, counselor, or administrator present.

Since the Franklin County District Attorney declined to prosecute anyone in this case, I decided something had to be done. Not that I had any idea where to start. What could an $11^{th}$ grade girl do to get the authorities to recognize they had committed a tragic error by allowing those responsible for a fellow student's death to go unpunished?

The school board of Franklin School District requires a graduation project from all students, and this book represents many more than the 60 hours of community service necessary to fulfill that mandate. In support of this fact I have kept a log. More than 200 hours were spent putting this project together.

I want to thank the teachers and administrators who signed my grad project time sheets. They patiently sat through the interviews and were helpful keeping order in a few cases. Of course, a special thank you goes out to Mr. Flory, my teacher and grad project advisor. He got me started and assisted in getting interviews with many of the key professionals connected to this case. Without Mr. Flory's help, I probably would have been dismissed as "just some kid". When doubts crept in, he was always there for me as a sounding board and source of encouragement. I sincerely appreciate his patience.


*Mary-Ellen Gerhard*

## Case Overview

Ashley White's family moved from South Carolina to Pennsylvania in the summer before he entered fifth grade in Franklin School District. Because of his musical talent, his first friends in Pennsylvania were all in band and chorus. Among those friends was an intelligent and talented girl by the name of Paisley Wahr. Paisley and Ashley were best friends, to the extent that Ashley felt comfortable confiding his deepest insecurities, hopes and dreams with her. Beyond Paisley, Ashley had three, perhaps four, close friends. Some people I have talked to saw as a "loner" or "lonely". When I pressed these people as to whether Ashley came across as a "brooding, sullen, angry, creepy, negative, or suicidal type", the answer was always a resounding no. However, for various reasons, mostly of the only-skin-deep-variety, he had low self-esteem, due to a severe case of acne in eighth and ninth grades. This self-consciousness resulted in being regarded by many as "a shy person". Paisley told me that Ashley was "particularly diffident and nervous around girls he found attractive". Nevertheless, this timidity did not keep him from excelling in other areas.

Ashley was a high achiever, academically speaking. His parents proudly showed me all of his marks from fifth through twelfth grades: all A's. Prior to his death he was on track to have the fourth highest GPA at Franklin. He made high honors from 8th grade forward, and, according to his teachers, friends and acquaintances, showed outstanding potential as a writer. He enjoyed writing and did so voluminously; going far beyond what was required for any given class where writing was involved in any way. Everyone close to him expected great things in his future, and he was clearly breaking out of his shell and experiencing newfound confidence

Of course, Ashley's life ended abruptly in an apparent act of suicide by motor vehicle. But how did he come to that emotional nadir?

According to Paisley Wahr, it was during the first week of February of their senior year, when Ashley admitted having a crush on one of Franklin's most popular and attractive girls. Like some kind of sweet, designer perfume, Mary Margaret Dolce was known to all by the monogram: M&M.

Ashley's confession was met by encouragement by Paisley. At lunch that day Paisley reminded Ashley of an up-coming opportunity to put action behind his words. As a fundraiser for the senior trip, student council would be running a flower and card delivery service on Valentine's Day. Students could buy white, yellow or red roses which represented differing sentiments. Paisley told Ashley to send M&M a red rose and to attach something nice he had written, along with an invitation to go out on a date to a movie.

Paisley went on to explain that Ashley's chances were actually just as good as anyone else's because of M&M's father. Mr. Dolce, also the head football coach at Franklin, was a very intimidating "old school" type dad. His daughter could only date if that boy had the guts to come to *him* and ask permission. In jest, although nobody could tell if he was kidding or not, Coach Dolce would often warn players on his team of the terrible things he'd do to them if he discovered someone taking his daughter out behind his back. Consequently, M&M didn't date. Even the most popular guys were afraid of Mr. Dolce, and that's the way he liked it.

M&M's untouchable status was magnified by her stunning physical attributes.

Of course, Ashley protested to his friend that he wasn't only interested in M&M because she's the "hottest girl in the entire school." He saw how "Sweet, kind and accepting of others" she was. Among all the pretty and popular girls, he insisted, "She was the only one with a heart".

After Paisley told him to "Put up or shut up", he looked her straight in the eyes and proclaimed, "I'm gonna do it."

At that point, he made some odd reference to Adam Levine and some skin care product, after which Paisley playfully dismissed him and he got up and left. She was left with the impression he was headed to the Valentine's Day table set up in the main hallway. He was brimming with confidence.

He did, in fact, pay to have a single red rose delivered to M&M, along with a simple note. He did not sign his name.

Observing from a safe distance, Ashley witnessed her positive reaction. During the day she bragged about it to her friends. With a big smile on her face, she showed it to everyone. Seeing M&M's delight, Ashley decided to do it again.

The second time it was just a poem written on a folded up piece of paper. He went to school early in order to deliver the poem without being seen by others. He used the horizontal air vents to slip it into her locker.

M&M's reaction was unmistakably positive. In fact, she even created and affixed a little "Mailbox" sign to her locker door, accompanied by a smiley faced emoticon with a red arrow pointing to the slats.

Of course, Ashley kept it up. He kept the notes and poems coming over the next 2 months.

During the second week of May one of M&M's friends, Brenda, happened to be at school extra early to hand in an overdue project. Brenda was walking down the mostly dark hallway when, from a distance, she noticed someone standing by M&M's locker. She stealthily retreated to the nearest corner of an intersecting hallway. Brenda got a good look at Ashley's face. She didn't know him, but she knew who he was and knew she could ID him later. She also noticed he was having difficulty slipping a larger-than-usual note into M&M's locker, so she made a noise designed to spook Ashley off before he could get the note into the locker.

He ran down the hallway in the opposite direction from the noise, and in his panic left the note behind, half protruding from the locker vent. She strolled to M&M's locker and pried the note loose from the slat, pocketing it for future use.

Brenda knew how to best make use of this discovery. Her plan was to wait for the most impactful moment to reveal this juicy piece of information to M&M. She wanted to divulge the truth when just the right people were there to see M&M squirm. I use the word *impactful* in this case because Brenda chose to tell her group of friends at a moment—and in a manner—intended to maximize their negative reaction.

She revealed the truth about M&M's secret admirer during lunch on May 13, but she didn't just come out with it. Rather, she started off by purposefully embarrassing one of her friends by telling a lie. You see, Brenda knew that one of her friends, Ty, had had a major crush on M&M for years, and she used this information to show everyone the latest anonymous note.

According to several witnesses, Brenda dramatically stood up, pulled the note out of her pocket, and proceeded to insist that *Ty Weiser* as the secret admirer and the source of the notes. She retold the story of what she had seen by M&M's locker, but at first led M&M and all of their friends seated at the lunch table, to believe she had seen Ty attempting to deliver the note. Keep in mind that Ty Weiser was actually sitting at the same table when Brenda did all this.

Once Brenda had created as much awkward embarrassment for Ty and M&M as possible, she abruptly retracted her accusation, and pointed across the lunchroom at Ashley White. As she identified him she also describing him as some sort of sick, twisted, perverted stalker. She threw in a few wild stories about how he had been following M&M around for months too. With this last tidbit she intended to spark a macho response from the guys—and it worked. Within minutes the guys were seriously discussing how they'd teach this creepy stalker a lesson he'd never forget.

Also present at the table was Brenda's boyfriend, Marty. He quickly came up with several retaliatory measures for possible use on Ashley, each based on his extensive repertoire of physical and mental bullying. The boys doubled over in laughter as they reviewed their prior misdemeanors and felonies. They had gotten away with savage practical jokes and other forms of "accidents" for years. For example, Marty and his friends even caused their 8th grade teacher serious physical harm once upon a time. They decided it would be funny to re-use that same old prank as a special "bonus" for Ashley.

That same weekend Marty threw a party at his house. Afterwards, he disclosed a detailed plot to his inner circle of friends. Although this "practical joke" was clearly designed to cause physical pain, the main purpose was to publicly humiliate Ashley and to potentially get him arrested and/or expelled from school.

On Monday the plan went into action.

By way of two eyewitnesses, and several legal and medical experts, it will be established that one of these conspirators spiked a carton of chocolate milk that Ashley thought had been sent to him by an appreciative M&M. They set Ashley up with this delivery, tricking him into believing M&M had finally figured out that he was her secret admirer—and was *happy* about it. It will be shown that this chocolate milk was laced with a powerful party drug, for the purpose of making a fool of him in class and causing susceptibility to the other ignominious experience they had set up for him in the class immediately following lunch.

Marty and his malicious coterie used Ashley's most lovey-dovey poem to M&M, blew it up to poster size, added his name in bold letters at the bottom, and pinned it high up on a bulletin in a spot designated by the teacher for the "Poem of the Week". This bulletin board was intended for students who were comfortable posting their work for all to see. At the start of class on Mondays, the teacher typically asked the contributor to read out loud what they had posted. Extra credit was assigned to these brave students.

This bulletin board was approximately 8 feet up on the window side wall of the classroom, just beyond the teacher's desk, and directly next to a tall, metal, filing cabinet. Normally the teacher kept a chair directly beneath the "Poem of the Week" bulletin board because she was a mere inch over five feet tall. Marty and his buddies incorporated this chair into their hateful slapstick routine by using the screwdrivers of a Swiss Army knife to loosen the screws—just so. They pinned the poster on the bulletin board, as high as they could reach, and then they slid the rigged-to-collapse chair back in place. The conspirators knew the classroom was always open during lunch period, as many students needed access to it to store book bags that couldn't possibly fit in their narrow lockers. They were able to stage the classroom because two or three of them left the lunch room, pretending to need to use the restroom during the last ten minutes of the period.

Marty's plan even included utilizing two of the girls as lookouts posted outside of the classroom doorway, and, if necessary to create distractions to keep Ashley and/or their teacher in the hallway until their depraved mission was accomplished.

Unfortunately for Ashley White, Marty's plan went off without a hitch.   When the teacher entered the classroom she noticed the poster straightaway and called upon Ashley to share what he had posted.  Of course, Ashley was horrified to see what poem had been posted in his name.

According to the teacher, and all of the innocent students in the classroom, Ashley leapt to his feet and careened across the room with reckless abandon. Some told me that he was screaming, while others reported that it was more like a "desperate groan".  In any case, when Ashley jumped up on the chair in an effort to rip the poster off the wall, it collapsed and he came crashing to the floor after striking his head on the corner of the filing cabinet.

Ashley was out cold. He didn't move.  Many students present thought he was dead. At least one sicko who was part of this "practical joke" laughed out loud and texted others about how funny she thought it was while Ashley lay unresponsive on the floor.

The teacher took action quickly, checking for vitals, calling the nurse, and commanding the students to be silent and remain in their seats.  A few minutes later, Ashley sat up suddenly. Most witnesses told me Ashley looked "insane" or "out of his mind".  The teacher and nurse saw it the same way.  They tried to be helpful, to calm Ashley down, but there was no consoling him. He launched into an expletive filled tirade against those he suspected of doing this to him. Everyone was shocked, as they had never even heard him swear once before in all the time they knew him.

When the nurse became insistent that Ashley sit down and let her check his pupils, he adamantly refused. When she next moved to the classroom phone and verbalized the need to call an ambulance, Ashley screamed and took off down the hallway at top speed, leaving the entire classroom in stunned silence.

The nurse then raised the principal on her emergency Walkie Talkie, concerned Ashley "wasn't in his right mind" and "might harm himself". Apparently the principal and guidance counselor sprang to action immediately because they intercepted Ashley by the main entrance doors within a couple of minutes, where they were able to momentarily get Ashley to calm down enough to temporarily divert him from his intention to go to his car and drive away from the school.

In the meanwhile the ambulance had been called and was on its way, when Ashley, now seated in the guidance sweet, became infuriated and crazed again, and succeeded in running out of the building. Moments later, everyone in the school heard him peeling out of his parking space and speeding across the lot to the exit.

Sadly, the local police, who had also been notified of the situation and were on the lookout for Ashley's Dodge Daytona, didn't locate him until it was too late. About 20 minutes later Ashley was driving on an isolated country road and apparently decided to kill himself by crashing his car into a telephone pole at approximately ninety miles per hour.

As the interviews will demonstrate, although Marty was the brainchild of these criminal acts, several of his friends played critical roles. Without their direct or indirect involvement the full and terrible effects of this "practical joke" could not have been realized. Whereas some of these helpers should be considered *accessories before the fact*, others must be regarded as *felony accomplices*.

## A Call for Arrests and Charges

I am not a professional investigator, nor am I a District Attorney with power to bring charges or issue indictments against Marty and his cruel clique. Nevertheless, I set before the reader extensive interviews—and my analysis of them—with the hope of confirming the correctness of the charges I'm recommending.

Now that you have a general overview of what happened in this case, I ask you to seriously read the interviews and consider whether Marty Fine and any others involved should face arrest and criminal charges in relation to Ashley White's apparent suicide.

I contend that, minus their involvement, Ashley would still be alive. The interviews will prove *beyond a reasonable doubt* that the "practical jokes" involved in this case were intentional criminal acts. In fact, a *series* of criminal acts were committed by Marty Fine and several of his friends. When you finish reading this book, I'm convinced you'll come to the same conclusion: Ashley White would not have committed suicide, minus these criminal acts.

In terms of appropriate charges, I've done extensive research. Pennsylvania's criminal statutes are available online, along with explanations of their applications.

After careful consideration, I'm recommending the charges of **involuntary manslaughter** and **reckless endangerment**.

Here are the applicable laws and their definitions:

## PA Criminal Statutes (Title 18)

### § 2504. Involuntary manslaughter.

(a)  General rule—

A person is guilty of involuntary manslaughter when as a direct result of the doing of an unlawful act in a reckless or grossly negligent manner, or the doing of a lawful act in a reckless or grossly negligent manner, he or she causes the death of another person.

**Involuntary manslaughter** usually refers to an unintentional killing that results from recklessness or criminal negligence, or from an unlawful act that is a misdemeanor or low-level felony.

**Reckless Endangerment:** A person commits the crime of reckless endangerment if the person recklessly engages in conduct which creates a substantial risk of serious physical injury to another person. "Reckless" conduct is conduct that exhibits a culpable disregard of foreseeable consequences to others from the act or omission involved. The accused need not intentionally cause a resulting harm or know that his conduct is substantially certain to cause that result. The ultimate question is whether, under all the circumstances, the accused person's conduct was of that heedless nature

that made it actually or imminently dangerous to the
rights or safety of others

## Disclaimer

None of the interviewees was forced to participate. All participating students, teachers, administrators, and professionals, have confirmed the accuracy of my transcripts. Of course, the people interviewed do not necessarily agree with my analysis or conclusions.

# Duwain Williams

The following is the transcript of my interview with Duwain Williams, conducted in the guidance office of Franklin High School, Jedesdorf, PA

Date:  June 11, 2011
Time:  2:37-3:33 PM
Witnesses:  Mr. Roger D. Flory (Teacher).

**Mary-Ellen:**  How old are you, Duwain?

**Duwain:**  I'm 19.

**Mary-Ellen:**  You're a senior, right?

**Duwain:**  Yeah.

**Mary-Ellen:**  Who are your closest friends at Franklin High?

**Duwain:**  Ty, Trudy, Marty, M&M, and Brenda…well, sort of.

**Mary-Ellen:**  Why do you seem to hesitate when calling Brenda Waxman a friend?

**Duwain:**  Uh, well, sometimes she can be a real jerk to my girlfriend, Trudy.

**Mary-Ellen:**  Trudy Schroeder is your girlfriend?

**Duwain:** Yup.

**Mary-Ellen:**  Tell me more about how Brenda treats Trudy.

**Duwain:**  I don't know exactly how to explain it. Brenda can act like a snob.  That's it.  You know, sometimes she acts like a rich know-it-all and likes to make Trudy feel like she isn't good 'nough to hang with us.

**Mary-Ellen:**  Us?  Do you mean you and the other friends you mentioned?

**Duwain:**  Yeah.

**Mary-Ellen:**  Who is your best friend among the guys?

**Duwain:**  Ty, of course.

**Mary-Ellen:**  Ty Weiser?

**Duwain:**  Uh-huh.

**Mary-Ellen:**  Give me some background about you and Ty.  Why are you two closer than, say, you and Marty?  Haven't you and Marty been best friends since middle school?

**Duwain:**  You're right.  Me and Marty were closer back then.  We played basketball and football together since we were 9 or 10.  Marty quit sports after he didn't make the varsity basketball team our sophomore year. He played football that year, but only special teams. He used to be one of the best athletes back in middle school.  He dominated back then.  He was big and quick. He never says it, but he's the sorta guy who needs to be number one. Marty kinda stopped growing in 8th grade and we didn't. You know what I mean? When he wasn't the best any more, he just quit and went on to be the best at other stuff.

**Mary-Ellen:** And Ty?

**Duwain:** He was the opposite. He used to be quiet and kinda small in middle school. Ty grew like 6 inches and put on weight and strength and stuff. He's super popular too—now. That's not the way it use-ta be. Anyway, Ty turned into the best QB this school has ever seen.

**Mary-Ellen:** Well, I know you have some sort of football scholarship to a division one school, so you must be pretty good too.

**Duwain:** We won two district championships together, you know. The attention from recruiters Ty got for setting all those passing records helped me to get noticed too.

**Mary-Ellen:** Where are you and Ty going to college?

**Duwain:** We both got full rides to play football. He's going to 'The U' [Miami University, Florida] and I'm going to West Virginia.

**Mary-Ellen:** Let's get back to Marty for a minute. You said something about him being the sort of person who has to be 'number one'. Since he wasn't excelling in sports, is that why he got involved in student council and music?

**Duwain:** Yeah. He's always been really popular. He's always got something interesting going. He's a natural politician. He's usually the center of attention. Always has been. He's the smartest guy in the school.

**Mary-Ellen:** And the music?

**Duwain:** Now, the music thing really isn't a school thing. It's his own band, not some [expletive deleted] school musical [expletive deleted].

**Mr. Flory:** Enough with the language, Duwain. That's uncalled for...

**Duwain:** Sorry, Flo-man.

**Mary-Ellen:** Were you expressing your feeling about music at our school, or did you mean that was Marty's attitude?

**Duwain:** Marty's. I don't really pay any attention to that stuff and those people, so I really don't care.

**Mary-Ellen:** What about Marty? Does Marty care about 'those people'?

**Duwain:** Dude, I didn't mean it *that* way. I just don't hang out with *bandos*.

**Mary-Ellen:** And Marty?

**Duwain:** You know Marty.

**Mary-Ellen:** No. Not really.

**Duwain:**  *Everyone* knows Marty.  C'mon.  You know he ain't hangin' 'round with no *losers*.

**Mary-Ellen:**  Would he go out of his way to persecute '*losers*', as you call them?

**Duwain:**  Persecute?

**Mary-Ellen:**  Yeah, *per-se-cute*.  Would you and Marty pick on '*losers*'?

**Duwain:**  I never done *nothing* to any of them.

**Mary-Ellen:**  And Marty?

**Duwain:**  You know it.

**Mary-Ellen:**  Tell me.  Give me an example or two.

**Duwain:**  You really think I'm gonna rat out a friend? Besides, it was never anything serious.  Just pranks and [expletive deleted].

**Mr. Flory:**  Here we go again.  Mary-Ellen, perhaps this interview has gone on long enough…

**Duwain:**  Sorry.  It just slipped out.  She got me mad—talk'n like she's 'cusing me and all.

**Mary-Ellen:**  Really, Mr. Flory, it's OK.  I have more, important, questions.

**Mr. Flory:**  One more 'slip up', and we're done here. Got it?

**Duwain:** Yup.

**Mary-Ellen:** OK. Let's move on to more important things. I only brought it up because Ashley White was a 'bando'.

About Ashley...did you know he was crushing on M&M?

**Duwain:** Only after Brenda told everyone at lunch.

**Mary-Ellen:** At lunch? What day was that?

**Duwain:** I don't remember. That was last year.

**Mary-Ellen:** Well, tell me what you *do* remember about that lunch. Tell me what Brenda said or did.

**Duwain:** I wasn't pay'n too much attention to what was goin' on. It was the usual lunch period. Me and Ty were talking with Marty. I was sitting next to Trudy and stuff. Then, all of a sudden, Brenda starts goin' off.

**Mary-Ellen:** About what?

**Duwain:** She tosses some "secret admirer" note on Ty's lunch tray and starts accusing him of being the one writing all the other notes.

**Mary-Ellen:** You mean, Brenda was accusing Ty of writing the love notes to M&M?

**Duwain:** Yup. Everyone knew my boy had the hots for M. He always denied it 'cause he know M wasn't allowed to date nobody. Brenda kept teasing Ty until he broke, saying he liked M. Then as he's startin' to get red in the face and all, Brenda laughs and says it's NOT him.

**Mary-Ellen:** Sounds like it was a gotcha moment.

**Duwain:** No doubt. That's Brenda. Like I was sayin' before 'bout why Trudy and me sometimes don't consider her a close friend.

**Mary-Ellen:** I see. That makes sense. Go on. What happened next?

**Duwain:** Ty finally 'mitted it and then Brenda told us 'bout this weirdo stalking M. She pointed him out and said he's the one writing the creepy notes.

**Mary-Ellen:** How did Ty react to that?

**Duwain:** He got all quiet and stuff. But Marty started talkin' 'bout teachin' him a lesson for mess'n with M.

**Mary-Ellen:** What did Marty say?

**Duwain:** He was just jokin' about the 'good ol' days' back 'n 8$^{th}$ grade…givin' swirlys and wedgies and stuff.

**Mary-Ellen:** Did Marty suggest giving Ashley White a swirly or wedgie?

**Duwain:** We talked about it. All of us. We were joking around about it. It wasn't really serious at first, but Brenda kept sayin' stuff about the notes Ashley wrote—making it sound like he was a stalker.

**Mary-Ellen:**  Did Brenda call Ashley White a "creepy stalker?"

**Duwain:**  Yup.  A bunch a times.

**Mary-Ellen:**  Before, you said you didn't remember what day it was when this happened at lunch.  Could it have been a Friday?

**Duwain:**  I suppose.  It was in May for sure…before Marty's party.

**Mary-Ellen:**  The party was on Saturday, May 11.  I know because I have a copy of Marty's Facebook post. Take a look.  Remember this?


[Turn to the next page for the image]

**Duwain:** Yup. I remember people came up to Marty that day at lunch. They hadn't received the event invite and were asking for one. He turned most of 'em away.

**Mary-Ellen:** Did you and Trudy get an invite?

**Duwain:** 'course.

**Mary-Ellen:** You attended the party on Saturday the 11$^{th}$ ?

**Duwain:** Yup.

**Mary-Ellen:** Do you remember much about the party?

**Duwain:** Wutch-ya wanna know?

**Mary-Ellen:** First, there are some that say Mercedes Perez was at the party. Do you remember seeing her there?

**Duwain:** She's one of Trudy's friends from softball. If she had been there, I would have seen Mercedes. I was with Trudy the whole time 'cept for the very end after everyone else had lef'. If Mercedes was there, she musta been hidin' out.

**Mary-Ellen:** So you never saw her there?

**Duwain:** Nope.

**Mary-Ellen:** Did Marty and his band play at the party?

**Duwain:** For 'bout an hour. They were 'suppose to play longer but Marty and the other two guys in the band weren't getting along. They're always fightin' 'bout something.

**Mary-Ellen:** Do you know the other two members of Marty's band, EP?

**Duwain:** Earl and Brent? Nah. Druggies. Punks. I know 'em but don't hang. Can't see why Marty ever got in wit 'em. He's smarter than that. They broke up that night—for good.

**Mary-Ellen:** Druggies? I hear that there were drugs at Marty's party. Did Earl and Brent supply the drugs?

**Duwain:** Yup…'nother reason Marty kicked 'em out.

**Mary-Ellen:** Of the party or the band?

**Duwain:** Band.

**Mary-Ellen:** Did you see Earl or Brent dealing?

**Duwain:** Nah, but I heard they were.

**Mary-Ellen:** Who told you?

**Duwain:** Brenda and Marty. They said Earl and Brent were dealin' X.

**Mary-Ellen:** X, as in ecstacy? Did you or any of your friends do X that night or any other time?

**Duwain:** Man, we got scholarships. Me and Ty ain't messin' that up with no drugs. The others? Well, you know, that's their business. I ain't sayin'.

**Mary-Ellen:** You wouldn't want your girlfriend messing up her life with drugs would you?

**Duwain:** Nope. But I can't control her every move. We aren't married ya'know.

**Mary-Ellen:** So, you're saying that Trudy may have done X that night?

**Duwain:** I don't know. That's all I'm sayin', 'specially wit d' Flo-man here. No offense.

**Mr. Flory:** None taken.

**Mary-Ellen:** OK, let's put the drugs aside for a moment. You mentioned a bit back that you hung out at the party after everyone else had gone home. Are you saying that some of you stayed at Marty's house after the party was over? If so, who?

**Duwain:** Trudy, Brenda and M&M were inside Marty's house—in the basement. Marty's dad has this awesome movie room downstairs: a home theater setup with a 92-inch, flat screen TV. They have some serious money.

Me, Marty and Ty were outside sittin' 'round the fire pit in Marty's backyard. We talked about what we were going to do on Monday in Ms. Lehrer's class.

**Mary-Ellen:** You're talking about what you guys were going to do to Ashley to teach him a lesson, right? What was the plan?

**Duwain:** Marty said we should unscrew a chair and have it collapse on Ashley like we used to do back in middle school. We laughed a bit about the time Marty unscrewed Mr. Krei's swivel chair in 8th grade science. One day, back then, Marty brought in a knife with a screwdriver on it and loosened the chair up—just enough to keep it together, but so that it would c'lapse when Mr. Krei came into class and sat down. Dude, Krei broke his backside bone thing.

About the plan on Saturday night for Ms. Lehrer's class, I don't remember much 'cept Marty wanted me to keep watch for Ms. Lehrer. He wanted me to warn him and stuff if she was commin'. Marty and Ty were gonna loose' the screws on a chair and put up a poster with one of Ashley's creepy poems on it for M&M. Marty wanted to 'barrass him real good.

**Mary-Ellen:** Now, let's talk about Monday in Mr. Lehrer's English class. Did you guys go ahead with your plan from Saturday night? What happened in class, exactly?

**Duwain:** After lunch we went to English. The room was open and Ms. Lehrer was out in the hallway talking with Trudy and Brenda. I guarded the door, and Marty and Ty pinned the poem to the bulletin board. The poster was way up. It was out of reach unless you stood on the chair. Marty or Ty unscrew'd the chair. If anyone'd stand on it or sit on it…it'd c'lapse.

Then, when class started, Ms. Lehrer noticed the poem on the poster with Ashley's name on it and asked him to read it to the class.

**Mary-Ellen:** How did Ashley react to that?

**Duwain:** He freaked out. He ran to the chair and jumped up. The chair fell apart and he came down wit it.

**Mary-Ellen:** Was he hurt?

**Duwain:** He was stunn'd or something. Then he looked upset—embarrassed and piss'd.

**Mary-Ellen:** What did Ms. Lehrer do?

**Duwain:** She was buggin'. Ashley was on the floor. I think she thought it was serious. She called the nurse and all. It looked worse than it probably was.

**Mary-Ellen:**  Is it true that you—and others in the class—were laughing at Ashley when he fell?

**Duwain:**  Yeah, I was laughin'.  Not as much as some others, but I was.  It did look funny—*like slapstick or something.*  It didn't seem like he was *really* hurt— probably just his pride.  Ashley was upset, but not really hurt from the fall— just 'barrassed.

**Mary-Ellen:**  Did Ashley say anything after he fell?

**Duwain:**  He sat up and then got up, cursin' up a storm.  Pointing fingers at us and screaming.  I mean, really screaming angry. He looked crazy in the eyes.  He actually looked *high* or something.  You know…*whacked.*  When the nurse showed up he took off—down the hall.  She chased after.  Ms. Lehrer did too.

**Mary-Ellen:**  With the teacher out of the room and Ashley gone, what did the others say and do?

**Duwain:**  I don't remember what they said.  Some were laughing, like I said before.  A couple of the girls were upset and concerned for Ashley.

**Mary-Ellen:**  By a "couple of the girls" do you mean Trudy, Brenda and M&M?

**Duwain:**  Nah.  First off, M&M wasn't in that class with us.  Trudy was a little upset.  Brenda was trippin' with Marty about it.  They couldn't stop laughing.  Ty and Marty high-fived each other.  That's 'bout all I remember.

**Mary-Ellen:** So which girls were upset?

**Duwain:** I don't know their names. They're the ones who hang with Ashley and stuff.

**Mary-Ellen:** Did these girls get angry at you guys for what you did to Ashley?

**Duwain:** I don't think they knew about the chair and poem.

**Mary-Ellen:** I almost forgot a question. I skipped it before when we were talking about drugs at Marty's party. I found out from Mr. Denker that Trudy sent him a letter about her and her friends doing drugs. Here let me read it out loud for you:

> Mr. D,
>     It seems a little weird to use this *questions box thing* to ask you a question, but I can't just walk into your office.
>     This past year me and my friends have been taking these pills called "rolls". They come in many different varieties, such as "Green CK's", "Pink Panthers", "Buddas". They have a little picture on them that goes along with the name. Most of my friends haven't even heard of them before and I was just wondering if you had. I was also wondering if you could tell me what is in them. They make your vision jump around and your sense of touch really intense. You're numb until you touch something or something touches you, then you can feel it through your entire body.

And I always tell people how much I love them, even if I don't like the person.

Everyone thinks these pills are harmless and I feel like I could stop at any time. Still, you told me once that I could talk to you about any problems I was having and that you would keep it confidential. Could I come down to see you this afternoon?

Trudy S.

**Duwain:** What!? She didn't write that. She's totally creeped out by Mr. D because he always tried to come across like he was cool and stuff. I think just 'cause he's young he thinks girls like him. Mr. D acts strange 'round pretty girls and all. Someone should probably look into how many times he tries to get girls into his office. Trudy is creeped out by the way Mr. D looks at her. It's awkward. She would *never* go and talk to him alone.

Mr. Flory, Mr. D should be suspended or maybe even lose his job for not stopping Ashley from leaving school—the principal too.

**Mr. Flory:** Are you serious? I've never heard any other student talk about him that way.

**Duwain:** Now you have. Dude, he's Mackin' on the hotties all the time.

**Mr. Flory:** I'll talk to the principal about it.

**Mary-Ellen:** Are you suggesting that Mr. D made up the note just to get your girlfriend in his office?

**Duwain:** Uh-huh.

**Mary-Ellen:** But what about what Brent and Earl say about Trudy and you guys?  They say that you guys do Ecstasy and probably put X in Ashley's drink that day at lunch.

**Duwain:** C'mon.  Fo-real?  You believe *them*?  They just savin' their own, uh…you know what I'm sayin' Mr. Flory.  They just blame'n Marty and Trudy, and me, since they probably put X in Ashley's chocolate milk themselves.

**Mary-Ellen:** I didn't mention anything about chocolate milk, Duwain.  How did you know it was *chocolate milk*?

**Duwain:** Just guessin'…Ashley was always drinkin' chocolate milk.

**Mary-Ellen:** Did you sit with, or even close to Ashley, at lunchtime? Do you ever talk to him at school?

**Duwain:** I don't like the 'tude, girl—'cusen me again.

**Mary-Ellen:** Well, tell me then, why would Brent and Earl put X in Ashley's chocolate milk? What did they have against Ashley?

**Duwain:** I-d'no.  These rock star wannabe's pick on geeks and nerds every day.  They haten' anyone who likes school—like Ashley.

**Mr. Flory:** Mary-Ellen, you wanted me to tell you when an hour's up. Time's almost up.

**Mary-Ellen:** OK. That's all I need.

**Duwain:** Hey, Flo-ster, will you sign my sheet for me? I'm getting' credit for this too.

**Mr. Flory:** Sure, pass it over.

## Commentary on the Duwain Williams Interview

Looking back, I'm confident that starting with Duwain Williams was the right choice. He was a participant and witness to the most essential elements of the crime. He's somewhat of a "weak link" among Marty's inner circle of friends, because he a lot to lose—a football scholarship to the University of West Virginia. I don't mean to suggest that he cracked or broke down during the interview, but I was able to "push his buttons" to get him to reveal more than he probably intended.

Duwain came across as a follower. Although he was definitely territorial in the protection of some of his friends, he doesn't seem to have contributed in any significant way to the plan to humiliate Ashley. It's likely he egged Marty and others on, never imagining the consequences. Duwain was swept along by events. He got caught up in a passive way with the plan. Why? Probably because it seemed funny to him at the time, and he enjoyed feeling like he was part of an elite and powerful clique.

Duwain adamantly denied involvement in prior practical jokes perpetrated by Marty; nevertheless, it didn't ring true. Perhaps you had to be there to see his face to understand this, but despite his reluctance to give details, his eyes and expressions showed me that he had vivid and perhaps enjoyable memories of these prior bullying incidents. He was clearly present when they occurred.

Although it's possible that his refusal to provide details is just a matter of avoiding implicating himself, I don't think this is the case. More likely, he was involved, just not directly or as the "ideas man".

This assessment certainly holds true in the case at hand. He was present as the plan was concocted by Marty and Brenda. He was there during lunch when Ashley was drugged. He was there, in the classroom, running interference for Marty and Ty so they could set up the poster and rig the chair to collapse. He never spoke up— or out—about it. At no point in the process did he object. However, he did object to the corrupting influence of Marty and Brenda when it came to drug use by his girlfriend, Trudy.

I tend to believe Duwain when he says he was not using or distributing drugs. In this regard, he did express what felt to me like genuine concern for Trudy, who he admitted was experimenting with illegal substances. Although he undoubtedly knew Marty was a drug dealer, I find it curious that Duwain was still somewhat protective of Marty during the interview, in the sense that he was willing to implicate Marty's other band mates instead, Earl and Brent. The possibility that Marty might still "have something" on Duwain seems likely to me. What that might be, I don't know.

On the other hand, I was surprised by the *intensity* of Duwain's distaste for and distrust of Marty's girlfriend, Brenda. Only after finishing the rest did this aspect of Duwain's interview make any sense to me. He clearly sees Brenda as a vicious person who looked down on others. I suspect his view of Brenda stems from the weird relationship between Brenda and Trudy.

Apparently Brenda could be quite cruel and demeaning to Trudy, and he didn't appreciate that.

I suspect this strange relationship had something to do with drugs. What exactly was involved I can only speculate about. The letter sent to the guidance councilor, Mr. Denker, *supposedly penned by Trudy*, is somehow connected.

Despite his resistance over certain questions and rough edges, I must admit to finding Duwain likable. He never seemed two-faced, like some of the other conspirators I've talked to and interviewed. And despite showing general prejudice toward others who don't fit into his world, like Ashley White, this is not proactive malice. While he probably sees himself as someone who isn't prejudiced against others, it also felt like he has a limited notion of the concept. For example, I'm not convinced he ever considered his assumption about Ashley being a "creepy stalker" was a form of prejudice. Brenda suggested this "creepy stalker" narrative about Ashley and Duwain ate it up without question and was eager to jump on the bullying bandwagon. When a person seeks to punish someone else before any evidence is in, what else is that other than prejudice?

## Ty Weiser

The following is the transcript of my interview with Ty
Weiser, conducted in room 104 at Franklin High
School, Jedesdorf, PA.

Date: June 12, 2011
Time: 2:40-3:20 PM
Witness: Mr. Roger D. Flory (Teacher).

**Mary-Ellen:** Ty, how old are you? You're a senior
this year, right?

**Ty:** I'm 18. Graduation is next week.

**Mary-Ellen:** I talked to your friend Duwain,
yesterday. He said that you two are best friends. Is
that true?

**Ty:** Definitely.

**Mary-Ellen:** What about a girlfriend?

**Ty:** Uh, well, it's kinda complicated.

**Mary-Ellen:** Go on. Duwain told me about M&M.

**Ty:** Yeah, M&M. True. I've liked M&M for 3 years
but I never told anyone except for Duwain. You see,
her dad is pretty intense, strict. He's our head football
coach. Coach Dolce doesn't permit M&M to date—
anyone, let alone **his** quarterback.

**Mary-Ellen:** Duwain said that Brenda tried to get you to admit to writing M&M all those secret admirer notes.

**Ty:** Yes. Brenda pulled a fast one on me to get me to admit I like M&M. She did it at lunch one day last year. I think it was in May. It was the same day she pointed out who Ashley White was.

**Mary-Ellen:** It was. Duwain confirmed that it was Friday, May 10, the day before Marty's party.

**Ty:** That's right.

**Mary-Ellen:** Tell me exactly what you remember Brenda saying or doing at the lunch table that day.

**Ty:** I was sitting across from M&M and next to Duwain. Out of the blue Brenda stands up and whips out a love poem form her pocketbook. She pointed at me and tossed it on my lunch tray. She started laughing and told everyone at the table she'd seen me that morning trying to put the love note in M&M's locker.

**Mary-Ellen:** Did you deny it?

**Ty:** I sure did. Nobody believed me though. I guess they really knew I had a massive crush on M&M. I'm sure I turned all shades of red when Brenda made the accusation too. It kinda game me away. After, I found out that they all thought I had been leaving these love notes and poems for months.

**Mary-Ellen:** But you didn't did you?

**Ty:**  No.  Ashley White was leaving them.

**Mary-Ellen:**  How did you find out it was actually Ashley White?

**Ty:**  After I was good and embarrassed, Brenda changed her story and told the truth.  She told us it was Ashley and she pointed him out at a table across the way.

**Mary-Ellen:**  Us?  Who did she tell?

**Ty:**  Besides me, it was Duwain, Marty, M&M and Trudy.

**Mary-Ellen**: All of your closest friends?

**Ty:**  Exactly.

**Mary-Ellen:**  When Brenda pointed out Ashley White, did you recognize him?  Was he a friend?

**Ty:**  Sure.  I recognized Ashley.  He was sitting at an almost-empty table.  It was him and, um, I think her name is Paisley.  Yeah, Paisley Wahr.  They're friends. I wasn't really friends with Ashley or Paisley.  Nobody at my table was close to him or Paisley.  He seemed like a nice guy.  Just a little creepy though…all those notes without puttin' his name to them.

**Mary-Ellen:**  When you first found out, did you think what Ashley had done was inappropriate? Did you think he was a stalker or might be dangerous to M&M?

**Ty:** Not really. Inappropriate? Yes. Stalker? Nah. But, Brenda and Marty seemed to think Ashley was dangerous. Just the thought of Ashley writing all of those love notes to M&M really seemed to make Brenda's skin crawl. I mean, she went on and on about how disgusting and weird it seemed to her. She kept repeating, "He makes my skin crawl".

**Mary-Ellen:** Did this revelation seem to make M&M's "skin crawl?"

**Ty:** Actually, no, she wasn't freaking out like Brenda. And when Brenda made a big deal about it and Marty said Ashley should be "put in his place", M&M told them to "knock it off". I think she kinda felt Sorry for Ashley. She had liked his notes and all—all along the way.

**Mary-Ellen:** You say M&M liked the notes. Isn't that because she had been thinking, hoping it was you all those months?

**Ty:** Yeah. I didn't know that the other girls—Brenda, and Trudy—had been telling M&M all along that it was probably me doing the love notes. I honestly didn't know that she thought that or I would have told her it wasn't me, starting with the first one on Valentine's Day last year.

**Mary-Ellen:** You were homecoming King to M&M's Queen this year. So I guess everyone assumed you two are a couple.

**Ty:** I know. People do…assume that, but we're not. Like I said about Coach Dolce and all.

**Mary-Ellen:** Understood.  Now, let's talk about what happened at the table at lunch after Brenda pointed out Ashley and told the truth.  What exactly did she say?

**Ty:** She pointed at him and…I don't remember her exact words, but she said something like, "Gross, he's a creepy stalker" and "He needs to be taught a lesson." No, scratch that last part.  That was actually what Marty and Duwain said *after* Brenda called Ashley a "creepy stalker" and claimed she had "noticed him following M&M around in the halls."

**Mary-Ellen:** Did you ever notice Ashley White "following them around" as Brenda claimed?

**Ty:** No, never.

**Mary-Ellen:** Why would Brenda lie about something like that?

**Ty:** I don't know.  She's like that.  She likes to stretch the truth to be the center of attention.  It's not the first time she to "put M&M in her place".

**Mary-Ellen:** In her *place*?

**Ty:** Uh-huh, in her place.  Brenda's jealous of the attention M&M gets from everyone.  They're friends, but Brenda sometimes can't take it that M&M is more popular.  Brenda would do stuff from time to time— to knock M&M down a peg or two.  It wasn't anything too serious, but it was usually mean-spirited.

**Mary-Ellen:** I get it. Now, I want to ask you about the party at Marty's house on Saturday night. Several people have said you and your friends were doing drugs, specifically X.

**Ty:** Am I going to get in trouble here, Mr. Flory? I don't want to lose my scholarship.

**Mr. Flory:** No. You're not going to get in trouble. But if you don't trust my word or the principal's word, just walk away or refuse to answer the question. Of course, I won't be signing your timesheet in that case.

**Ty:** OK. I'm not really concerned with me as much as getting Trudy or M&M in trouble.

**Mary-Ellen:** Why? Did they do X that night?

**Ty:** Ah…yeah. They each did one. Marty gave M&M another one, but she flushed it down the toilet after he walked away.

**Mary-Ellen:** Duwain said that Brent and Earl were the ones dealing X at Marty's party. Brenda has told people that Mercedes Perez was dealing it too. Who's telling the truth?

**Ty:** I like Marty and all. He's my friend. Truth? It was Marty. Mercedes wasn't even there that I can remember.

**Mary-Ellen:** Did you see Marty give M&M pills?

**Ty:** With my own two eyes.

**Mary-Ellen:** Are you sure you weren't already high at that point?

**Ty:** No. I wasn't high. No drugs. No booze. Nothing. I even encouraged M&M to flush it. *Ask her.*

**Mary-Ellen:** I will ask her…and Trudy too. She must have heard you tell M&M to flush the pill.

**Ty:** She did. Ask Trudy. She'll tell the truth.
**Mary-Ellen:** So you're absolutely sure it wasn't Brent or Earl or Mercedes?

**Ty:** Like I said before, Mercedes wasn't there. Brent and Earl may do pot, but not X. I know for a fact that they had a serious fight with Marty over the name of their band about X.

**Mary-Ellen:** What does *that* have to do with X?

**Ty:** The band name is EP. Surely you know that. Well, what does EP stand for?

**Mary-Ellen:** I don't know? Is it an EP-LP thing, like with old records and record players? The singles with Extended Play or the Albums or Long Play records?

**Ty:** Not even close. I can't believe you didn't hear about this?

**Mary-Ellen:** No. I'm interested to know. Just spit it out.

**Ty:** The band's initials stood for "Electric Potential" but Marty wanted it to secretly stand for "Ecstasy

Pilot." Calling the band "Ecstasy Pilot" was all Marty's idea. He's a dealer and he gets the stuff from his own parents.

**Mary-Ellen:** What? His parents?

**Ty:** *Ab-so-freakin'-lutely.* How many other parents make sure to "go away for the weekend" when their son wants to have a party at the house? How many parents make sure the house is well stocked with beer and porn for their son's parties?

**Mary-Ellen:** None.

**Ty:** See my point?

**Mary-Ellen:** Yes. Um, let me look through my notes. You got me off track. At the party...after the others had gone home, did you guys talk about what you were going to do "to teach Ashley a lesson" in class on Monday? Duwain said you guys talked about a plan to embarrass Ashley by putting up a poem of his to M&M and loosening a chair so he would fall. Is that accurate?

**Ty:** Yeah. Marty had a very detailed plan and we talked about what each person would do.

**Mary-Ellen:** You agreed to it...to play a part?

**Ty:** Yes.

**Mary-Ellen:** What was your part? How about Marty and Duwain?

**Ty:** To help Marty pin the poem up on the wall, then step down and let Marty unscrew the chair.  I placed the rigged chair under the poem after he was done.  Duwain kept the others away from us and stood guard in case Ms. Lehrer came in.

**Mary-Ellen:** What about Trudy, Brenda and M&M?

**Ty:** M&M wasn't in our English class.  She wasn't there at all.  Brenda and Trudy kept Ms. Lehrer out in the hallway…until Duwain signaled them he was done.

**Mary-Ellen:** How did they keep Ms. Lehrer in the hallway?

**Ty:** I think they asked her all sorts of questions about a term paper. I was inside the room, so I don't really know for sure.

**Mary-Ellen:** How did Ashley react when he spotted his poem on the wall?

**Ty:** As you might expect.  He blew a gasket.  He flew out of his desk and over to the wall and hopped on the chair to tear the poem down.  Ms. Lehrer actually saw it first and had drawn everyone's attention to it.  She thought Ashley wanted to share his work.  That's the usual way things are done with creative work on Monday's.

**Mary-Ellen:** Usual way?

**Ty:** Yeah, Ms. Lehrer has a place on the wall where students place their creative works and then share them on Mondays.  When she saw Ashley's name on the poem—Marty wrote it big in black magic marker—she asked Ashley if he would read the poem aloud.

**Mary-Ellen:** Duwain said he freaked at the sight of it. Can you describe how Ashley acted and what exactly he said?

**Ty:** Duwain's right. He fell as the chair collapsed under his weight. He crashed to the floor and was knocked out for a few minutes. When he woke up with all of us staring at him…he totally wigged out.

**Mary-Ellen:** Duwain said you guys were laughing at him when he fell. Is that true?

**Ty:** It did look funny, like something from the *Three Stooges.* Ashley was upset and embarrassed and yelled at us. He swore at us and said he hated us and "wasn't coming back".

**Mary-Ellen:** Duwain said that he thought Ashley might have been high on something. What do you think?

**Ty:** Duwain *did* say that to me too, right after Ashley ran out of the classroom. Others in the class said it too, like Marty and Brenda, and a few others. I don't think he was high as much as enraged. I kinda felt bad about it after he fell. I never wanted him to get hurt. I just thought it would be funny. He shouldn't have been stalking M&M.

**Mary-Ellen:** Did you think he was seriously injured due to the fall?

**Ty:** He hit his head on the way down. I heard it and saw his head kinda bounce off the filing cabinet. He hit the floor like a sack of potatoes and was out cold for a few minutes. At the time it crossed my mind he might have a concussion. When he woke up he had a wild look in his eyes. I think his pupils may have been different sizes. The black part of at least one of his eyes was *way big*.

**Mary-Ellen:** You could see his pupils? You must have been awfully close.

**Ty:** I was in the first seat next to where he fell on the floor. He sat up right in front of my desk, probably only three or four feet from me.

**Mary-Ellen:** Duwain said Ms. Lehrer was very concerned for Ashley and called the nurse right away. Is that the way you remember it?

**Ty:** Yes. Ms. Lehrer did call the nurse and the nurse came pretty quick. When the nurse came in the room, that's when Ashley went off on everyone and ran out screaming at the top of his lungs, "F this...and F that." Ms. Lehrer and the nurse ran after him. I don't know where he went after that.

**Mary-Ellen:** In the classroom, after they left, did anyone seem upset that Ashley might be hurt?

**Ty:** Yes, a few of Ashley's friends. I was upset and a bit in shock I think. It seemed unreal. I didn't say much. Brenda and Marty were talking but I don't remember what about.

**Mary-Ellen:** OK. When you talked to M&M next, what did she say about the whole thing? You told her what happened after school when you saw her...right?

**Ty:** She was very upset and concerned for Ashley. She was worried about him physically and mentally. She cried and said Ashley had really been sweet and not a stalker at all. She said he didn't deserve it. She was upset with me for helping. You can ask her, and she'll tell you, I apologized to her for being involved. She wanted to know where Ashley was, but I had no idea where he was.

**Mary-Ellen:** OK. I have two more questions. Look at this. It's a picture of a pocket knife. Duwain said Marty used a knife to loosen the screws on the chair, just like you told me a few questions ago. Is this the sort of knife Marty used?

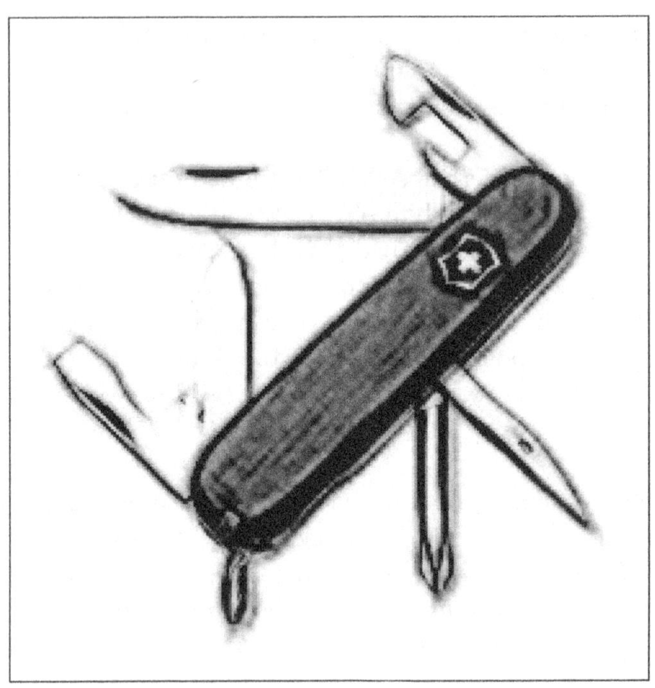

**Ty:**  Yes.  Marty used his Swiss Army knife with the Phillips head screwdriver attachment.

**Mary-Ellen:**  Think back to the lunch that same day. Did Marty ever leave the table and disappear for a while toward the end of the period?  If he did, how long was he gone?  How about M&M?  Did she ever leave the table with the chocolate milk she was giving to Ashley?

**Ty:**  Um, Marty went to the bathroom before the lunch period was over.  Yeah, it was close to the end of the period.  He never came back to the lunchroom prior to dismissal. Maybe he was gone a few minutes.

M&M was with me the whole time.  No, she didn't give Ashley chocolate milk.  Nobody at our table had chocolate milk, as far as I can remember.

**Mary-Ellen:**  OK, sorry, but I have a couple more quick questions now.

**Ty:**  Go ahead.

**Mary-Ellen:**  I'm trying to put things in order in my head and there's something that's bothering me about what you said about Marty going by himself to the bathroom early.

**Ty:**  Yeah, what about it?

**Mary-Ellen:**  If *you* pinned the poster up high on the wall, on the bulletin board, what did you stand on to reach that high?  I mean, you're tall and all, but you're not 8 feet tall.

**Ty:**  It must have been a stool or a different chair. I...don't remember.

**Mary-Ellen:**  Well, it couldn't have been the chair that Marty had already loosened the screws on, or it would have collapsed under your weight.  Right?  Or did you actually leave the lunchroom with Marty and go with him to Ms. Lehrer's room from the get-go?

**Ty:** No, like I said before, I didn't get there until the last possible moment.  Marty had unscrewed the chair but hadn't pinned up the poster yet, when I arrived.  I must have quickly pulled over a different chair or stool.

**Mary-Ellen:** Hold on, Ty. Mr. Flory, I'll have to play back the recording of this interview later to check, but I'm pretty sure Ty said, a while back, something like he "helped Marty pin the poem up and *then* stepped down to let Marty unscrew the chair". Does that sound right to you?

**Mr. Flory:** Honestly, I don't recall.

**Ty:** Well, I'll help you out...I *never* said that.

**Mary-Ellen:** OK, let's drop it and move on.

Did you see anyone at Ashley White's lunch table that day? Did you see anyone deliver a carton of chocolate milk to Ashley's table while he and Paisley were temporarily away?

**Ty:** Well, Mercedes Perez usually sits at the table next to Ashley's. She sits with the rest of the softball team—minus Trudy, of course. Trudy was with Duwain at our table. I've heard Mercedes does drugs, including ecstasy. I wasn't paying attention to Ashley's table at all. Honestly, I don't know. I do remember seeing him all happy at the end of the lunch period. I do remember seeing him talking with Paisley Wahr and him showing her the chocolate milk and the sticky note.

**Mary-Ellen:** What did he do with the milk carton and sticky note after lunch?

**Ty:** No clue. Sorry.

**Mary-Ellen:** I don't have any more questions.

## Commentary on the Ty Weiser Interview

When I first replayed my recording, in order to make a transcript of Ty's interview, what stood out to me was the fact that *he didn't actually believe Brenda's characterization of Ashley as a creepy, potentially dangerous, stalker.* Unlike Duwain who seems to have bought into Brenda's narrative, Ty never did. Still, he went along with Marty's plan to humiliate Ashley, even going so far as to actively participate in rigging Ms. Lehrer's classroom for the "practical joke". To me, his admission that he never regarded Ashley as some horrible, dangerous, stalker-guy makes his involvement even worse. Just like Duwain, Ty never attempted to dissuade Marty. He actively encouraged Marty, and admitted to being the one who pinned the poster up on the bulletin board. Of course, as he tells the story, Marty was alone responsible for unscrewing the chair, which brings me to the second major find of this interview.

Close the end of Ty's interview, there was some confusion on this above-mentioned matter. I could have sworn Ty initially said he *stood on the same chair* that Marty then unscrewed *after* Ty stepped down. Ty denied ever saying that. For the record, here is exactly what he is recorded saying:

> "To help Marty pin the poem up on the wall, then step down and let Marty unscrew the chair. I placed the rigged chair under the poem after he was done. Duwain kept the others away from us and stood guard in case Ms. Lehrer came in."

Clearly I was correct. Ty must have realized he had made a mistake, and been caught in a lie, so he changed his story. I believe he *did* leave lunch early and *was* in Ms. Lehrer's classroom with Marty the entire time.

Another important detail discovered in this interview involves Marty, Brent and Earl's band "EP". Apparently Marty's insistence that the initials of his band stood for "Ecstasy Pilot" rankled his band mates, who were two of the three original band members, and had named their band "Electric Potential". Marty was a late-comer to the band, and there was a significant falling out when Marty became a control freak determined to use the band as a front for his drug dealing. More on this tiff comes to the surface in my interviews with Brent and Earl.

Lastly, but perhaps most significantly, is who Ty *omitted mentioning* when I asked him questions about who was at his lunch table on the day of the prank. I was interested in finding out who could have delivered the chocolate milk spiked with ecstasy to Ashley's table. He thought it was important to mention that Mercedes sat at the next table over from Ashley, as if to suggest she had the opportunity without coming right out and accusing her. He also mentioned the people sitting at his own table during that window of opportunity when Ashley and his friend Paisley were away from their otherwise completely unoccupied table. Marty had supposedly already gone to the restroom, so he names Duwain, Trudy & M&M as still being there with him at the table at the time someone could have delivered the spiked chocolate milk. Notice, Ty never mentioned

Brenda.    As the reader will find, by way of the remaining interviews, Brenda *was* there.

Well, since Ty was already caught lying when he claimed not to have gone with Marty "to the restroom", it certainly could have been him making the delivery.    It's plausible he didn't depart for the "restroom" at the same time as Marty, but waited a few minutes before going into action.    Take a second look at what he told me, and notice the details he gives me—without being prompted by me to do so.

**Me:**
Did you see anyone at Ashley White's lunch table that day?  Did you see anyone deliver a carton of chocolate milk to Ashley's table while he and Paisley were temporarily away?

**Ty:**  Well, Mercedes Perez usually sits at the table next to Ashley's.  She sits with the rest of the softball team—minus Trudy, of course.  Trudy was with Duwain at our table.  I've heard Mercedes does drugs, including ecstasy.  I wasn't paying attention to Ashley's table at all. Honestly, I don't know.  I do remember seeing him all happy at the end of the lunch period.  I do remember seeing him talking with Paisley Wahr and him showing her the chocolate milk and the sticky note.

Notice how he adds the bits about Ashley's happiness and the sticky note.  If he "wasn't paying attention to Ashley's table at all" as he claims, how could he have seen this crucial detail?  Moreover, if he wasn't really there, as I now believe, how did he know about the sticky note at all?   Either way, his testimony is extremely suspect, and indicates some sort of prior knowledge about the delivery of the carton.

It is reasonable to suspect Ty or Brenda, *or both*, of delivering the spiked chocolate milk to Ashley's table.

# Earl Samuels

The following is the transcript of my interview with Earl Samuels, conducted in room 103 at Franklin High School, Jedesdorf, PA.

Date: June 13, 2011
Time: 3:00-3:30 PM
Witness: Ms. Strauss (Teacher).

**Mary-Ellen:** Earl, thanks for helping today. I promise I won't keep you long. I have about 6 questions for you, so you'll be out of here in no time. How old are you?

**Earl:** No problem. Like I said, I can stay until 3:30. I'm 17, soon to be 18 on the 20th.

**Mary-Ellen:** Great. You know I've spoken with others involved in this case about your band, "EP"…right?

**Earl:** Yes.

**Mary-Ellen:** What do the initials "EP" stand for?

**Earl:** Electric Potential.

**Mary-Ellen:** Not "Ecstasy Pilot"?

**Earl:** No, *Electric Potential.* The only dumb-[expletive deleted] who would say that are Marty, his [expletive deleted] and maybe his mind-strangled-by-his-jockstrap-buddy, Duwain.

**Ms. Strauss:** Earl, let's not ruin this with the language. I know you want to clear your name.  Speaking that way won't help.

**Earl:**  Point taken.  Continue.  Ask away, Mary-Ellen.  But, before you go on to another question, have you seen the EP poster Marty put together for the party at his house last May?  I want to show you something.  He designed it and posted it as part of a Facebook event invite.  He created this [expletive deleted]—not me...not Brent.  What I'm going to show you *proves* he's a liar about the band name controversy.  Do you have a copy on your iPhone?  Pull it up.  I play lead guitar and write music.  Marty-boy always acts like he's the 'promoter'.  He thinks he's "all that"...the 'brains'.

**Mary-Ellen:**  Yes, here it is.  What about it?

**Earl:**  Look at the small lettering...here in the bright light under the woman figure's feet.  It says "Ecstasy Pilot" right there...see it?

**Mary-Ellen:**  Wow, that's awfully small.  It's hard to read.

**Earl:**  Zoom in.  Look, you can see it clearly on mine.  The band broke up because he was out of control.  He's an X dealer—a filthy rich, spoiled, control freak jerk.

**Mary-Ellen:**  Was he dealing X at his party last May?

**Earl:** Of course.

**Mary-Ellen:** Did you have any? Or smoke pot at the party?

**Earl:** So, I have a reputation for smoking weed?

**Mary-Ellen:** Honestly? Yes.

**Earl:** You got me there … but no X. Brent either.

**Mary-Ellen:** OK. Let's move on. Did you know Ashley White? Did you or Brent have anything against him?

**Earl:** Where would you even get an idea like that? Um, let me guess...from Marty and Brenda...right? I didn't even know who Ashley was. I knew he was in my grade, but we never spoke in 4 years of high school. *Not once.*

**Mary-Ellen:** Someone told me that your girlfriend, Mercedes Perez, is the one dealing X. Is that true?

**Earl:** First off, Mercedes *isn't* my girlfriend. She's a friend. I would date her if she was interested, but she's not. She has a boyfriend at Drexel. Second, she's not an X dealer. She doesn't do drugs of any sort. Not even weed.

**Mary-Ellen:** At least one person, other than Marty and Brenda told me Mercedes was at Marty's party and was dealing X. One person told me she put a chocolate milk carton on Ashley White's lunch table on

Monday, May 13 too.  They are saying Mercedes spiked the carton with X.  Why would they make that up?

**Earl:** Who said that?  Unbelievable!  I swear to God she would never do anything like that.  She's got no reason.  No motive.  Go talk to the practical joker.  I'm outta here.

**Mary-Ellen:** Aw…really?  It's not my fault other people are saying these things.

**Earl:** Bye. Good luck.  I hope [expletive deleted] Marty and his lying, [expletive deleted] evil girlfriend end up in prison for life for what they did.  If this ever actually goes to court you can count on me to testify.  I'd love to help put them away.

**Ms. Strauss:** If you leave early you won't get your sheet signed.

**Earl:** Oh, well.  Later.

**Mary-Ellen:** Later.  But, please, just one more thing.

**Earl:** One.

**Mary-Ellen:** Did you take Mercedes to Marty's party?  Did you drive her home that night, early, before everyone else left?

**Earl:** Yes, she left real early.  As soon as we finished our set I drove her home.

**Mary-Ellen:** How did she get to the party in the first place?

**Earl:** She said Trudy drove her there. *Are we done now?*

**Mary-Ellen:** Done.

# Brent Card

The following is the transcript of my interview with Brent Card, conducted in the guidance office of Franklin High School, Jedesdorf, PA.

Date: June 14, 2011
Time: 2:40-3:13 PM
Witness: Mr. Roger D. Flory (Teacher).


**Mary-Ellen:** Tell me a bit about your band, "EP".

**Brent:** There's not that much to tell. I play bass. Earl plays lead. We've had a half dozen other guys play drums for us over the past 3 years and 2 different lead singers. Currently the band is re-forming under a different name because we gave Marty the boot. Our new band is tentatively called "Black Mercury", and Earl and I have been conducting try-outs for drummer and lead vocals for the last 3 months. Right now, the band is really just two guys who love to write music and lyrics. Two guys committed to making great music and hoping some day to get noticed.

**Mary-Ellen:** Why did you guys invite Marty to be part of the band in the first place? It sounds like you didn't really know him, going in.

**Brent:** The band has been together for a year and a half at that point and we couldn't find anyone to help us get the word out. We needed someone to help raise the band's profile. We never really liked Marty, but his popularity and online marketing skills were appealing.

We hoped he'd bring attention to the group, so we put up with him until the poster incident. We then realized he was using us to promote his real business—selling drugs. I suppose we made a devil's bargain for fame.

**Mary-Ellen:** A devil's bargain? That's pretty strong language.

**Brent:** Sounds extreme, I know. I'm not even a religious person, but that's how it seems looking back now. We knew Marty was a drug dealer and we took the risk of taking him on. He nearly destroyed our reputation by making everyone at Franklin believe we were dealing ecstasy. He helped to make us popular and then used our popularity to gain hundreds of regular customers for him...and his father.

**Mary-Ellen:** You are the second or third person to suggest that Mr. Fine is a drug dealer. Like father, like son?

**Brent:** It's the truth.

**Mary-Ellen:** So, are you saying that you looked the other way, knowing Marty and his dad were involved in illegal activities—for the sake of the possibility of getting a music contract?

**Brent:** You gotta understand, Marty's dad has all sorts of connections. He knows famous people like music producers, studio managers, etc. Mr. Fine has a good friend who actually owns a music label.

**Mary-Ellen:**  Tell me something about Marty before high school.  Everyone says he was and is the quintessential practical joker.  Is that true?

**Brent:**  Back in the middle school days I hung with Marty before he was "Mr. Popular." I saw him pull off some hysterical practical jokes.

**Mary-Ellen:**  Such as?

**Brent:**  You know…immature stuff, like putting itching powder in someone's gym shorts, or secretly spiking someone's hamburger or drink at lunch with laxatives, or putting Vaseline on a classroom doorknob to slime a teacher we didn't like, or unscrewing chairs and desks—just so—so it would stay together until someone sat on them…then *bang*—down they'd go in a heap.

**Mary-Ellen:**  He actually did these things to people?

**Brent:**  He did…and worse.

**Mary-Ellen:**  Do tell.

**Brent:**  I'll give you one more.  He would get a pass to the restroom during class so he could be alone and not get caught.  He would wrap clear tape around the mouth of the faucet like an invisible, upturned spout. When someone turned it on to wash their hands after using the urinals they would get sprayed with water. His hope was to get them in the crotch.  The idea was to get the nerds to look like they peed themselves.

**Mary-Ellen:** I'm more interested in knowing about how he used to unscrew desks and chairs. You actually saw him do that?

**Brent:** Sure, I saw him. He did it to my chair in Mr. Kimball's class in 7th grade! He claimed he didn't know I was going to sit in that particular chair, but I knew he meant to embarrass me. He did it to lots of the less popular kids. Marty would use his Swiss Army knife to unscrew students' and teachers' chairs and desk chairs so they'd collapse at the funniest times. In fact, one time he did it to your 8th grade teacher's rolling chair. I'm sure you remember Mr. Krei. He rolled from the back of the classroom to the front and the chair collapsed, catapulting the Krei-ster backwards, flipping him over on his rear end. The Krei-ster broke his coccyx. Nobody ever figured out who had done it and Mr. Krei thought the chair was faulty. I heard that since he couldn't teach that he sued the school district or something.

**Mary-Ellen:** I heard that too. It's an urban legend. I spoke with the principal and it's *not* true. Mr. Krei was only a few months away from retiring. He had enough sick days saved up to simply retire before the end of the year.

**Brent:** Oh. Marty would be disappointed to hear that.

**Mary-Ellen:** I want to get back to the band and drug question again. Did you ever witness Marty doing ecstasy or dealing it?

**Brent:** I have never seen Marty do ecstasy. I've heard him talk about it. I've seen him handing it out to others and taking money for it. That makes him a dealer in my mind. Marty loves to brag and exaggerate a lot too, so it was hard to tell how deep he was really into the stuff or how many seriously bad people he really knew or dealt with. Again, he bragged about his "connections" constantly. At the time my attitude was, he can do whatever he wants on his own time, as long as it doesn't hurt me or the band.

The problem was that he was promoting the band as a way to get more people to buy ecstasy. He was even advertising EP by suggesting those initials stood for "Ecstasy Pilot" rather than "Electric Potential". He even put up promotional posters at school with phrases and images suggesting we were into ecstasy. I'm glad the teachers never noticed or we could have been in real trouble.

Earl told me you've seen it. Take a look at the Facebook event invitation post for his party on Saturday, May 11 of last year. In the top, right, he put the words: "Rolling, rolling…rolling along." Everyone knows "rolling" is a code word for doing X. When I found out about what he had done it was the last straw. I kicked him out of the band and told him we were on longer friends.

We haven't talked since. Earl hasn't talked to Marty either.

**Mary-Ellen:** I'm going to ask you a question I asked Earl. At least one person, other than Marty and Brenda, told me Mercedes Perez was at Marty's party and was dealing X. One person told me Mercedes put a chocolate milk carton on Ashley White's lunch table on Monday, May 13 too. They are saying Mercedes spiked the carton with X. Why would they make that up?

**Brent:** No way. Mercedes is not a drug dealer. In fact, she's the only person I know at Franklin who's probably totally clean. Even I will admit—as I'm sure Earl will—that I've done some Chronic from time to time. Mercedes doesn't even drink.

## Commentary on the Earl Samuels and Brent Card Interviews

The interviews of these two founding members of what came to be considered by most students at Franklin HS as "Marty's band" is important primarily because their struggle with Marty over the identity of their band, EP.

Both guys agree Marty Fine is a smug, spoiled brat who's a major drug source, pusher and dealer. His drug of choice is ecstasy, which he even codified when he tried to change the meaning of his band's name from "Electric Potential" to "Ecstasy Pilot". The image Marty created for the Facebook event invitation he sent out to hundreds of students at Franklin is powerful evidence of his not-so-secret way of notifying people that this drug would be available at the party held at his house on the Saturday before Ashley's death. For these reasons, Marty and his friend's attempt to smear Mercedes Perez as the drug dealer who spiked Ashley's chocolate milk *fails*.

The credibility of Earl and Brent's responses to my questions is reinforced by the fact that they make no attempt to hide their own faults and wrongdoing. In this respect, Brent's admission to being involved in the early year of Marty's bullying is very instructive. Consider what Marty got away with already in 7th grade when he pulled the same chair-rigged-to-collapse stunt!

# Mary Margaret Dolce

The following is the transcript of my interview with Mary Margaret Dolce, conducted in the guidance office of Franklin High School, Jedesdorf, PA.

Date: June 15, 2011
Time: 2:40-3:28 PM
Witness: Mr. Roger D. Flory (Teacher).


**Mary-Ellen:** How old are you M&M?

**M&M:** 18

**Mary-Ellen:** Obviously, this is your senior year, right?

**M&M:** Yes, graduation is next week.

**Mary-Ellen:** Where are you going to college?

**M&M:** I'm going to NYU to study journalism.

**Mary-Ellen:** Impressive.

**M&M:** Thanks.

**Mary-Ellen:** OK. Let's get down to business. Think back to Valentine's Day, last year. At school that is. Did you receive a special, anonymous, love note?

**M&M:** Yes, I did. I remember very well.

**Mary-Ellen:** When I texted you last, I asked you to bring that note. Do you have it? If so, would you mind describing it or reading it into the record?

**M&M:** No problem. It's a plain white card with a short message written in a bold, red, Valentine's Day font…see?

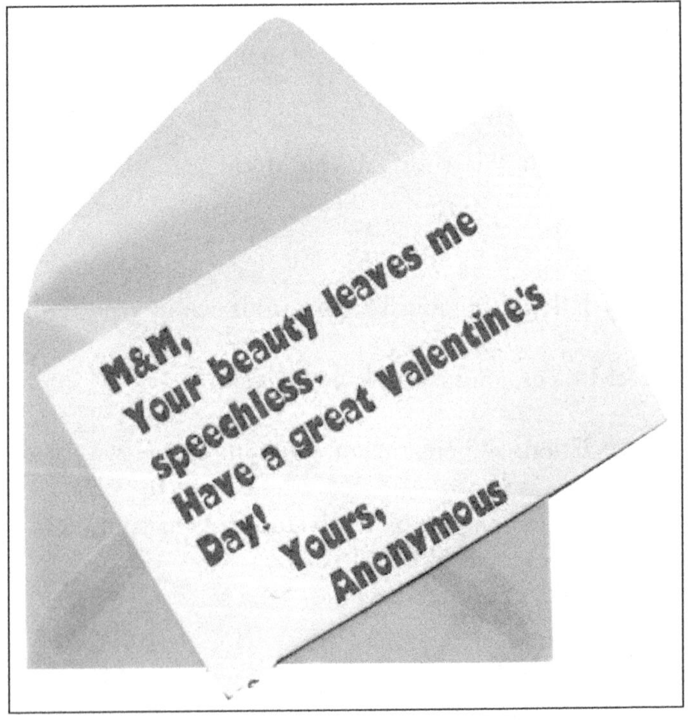


**Mary-Ellen:** How did you feel about receiving this?

**M&M:** I was thrilled. It's sweet. Someone was too shy to put their name on to it.

**Mary-Ellen:** Did you have any inkling about who sent it?

**M&M:** I didn't. Brenda and Trudy sure did. They were one hundred percent sure it was from Ty. You know, Ty Weiser. They teased me—in a good way—about it, saying Ty was "soooo sweet," "soooo adorable," "soooo romantic."

**Mary-Ellen:** Did you suspect it was Ty after Brenda and Trudy's reaction? Also, would you have thought Ty had sent the note if they had *not* suggested he did?

**M&M:** No, I really only came to believe the "anonymous romantic" was Ty after hearing Brenda and Trudy repeating their suspicion the entire day.

**Mary-Ellen:** It sounds as if you didn't really believe it was Ty, even though you wanted to believe it was Ty. Is that the way it was?

**M&M:** Well, I *wanted* to believe it. I had never seen this "soft side" of him. You understand, I'm not the only girl who thinks he's the best looking guy at Franklin, but the romantic idea of the hottest guy also being so sensitive was hard to resist. .

**Mary-Ellen:** Other than what you've already mentioned, was there anything Brenda and Trudy said or did to convince you Ty had written the anonymous note?

**M&M:** I suppose they pointed out how shy he always was around me, particularly after the Valentine's Day note had been delivered. Trudy swore Duwain had "spilled the beans" to her about Ty crushing on me and writing the note.

**Mary-Ellen:**  Be honest.  Did you *want* it to be Ty?

**M&M:**  Oh, yeah.  He's a hottie.  Like I said before, it was nice to think the cutest guy had sent me a note and rose.

**Mary-Ellen:**  There was a rose too?

**M&M:**  Yes.  I suppose I forgot to say that.

**Mary-Ellen:**  Did Brenda or Trudy approach Ty that day and try to get him to 'fess up?

**M&M:**  Yes. Right away they went over to him at his locker and playfully teased him about it until he blushed. The *way* he denied it made us believe he was embarrassed for getting caught.

**Mary-Ellen:**  What did you *personally* make of his reaction?  I'm not asking about Trudy and Brenda's reaction, just yours.

**M&M:**  Truth?  He looked so adorable.  He was so shy about it.  It was totally unlike the way he usually acted. He acted like a cute little boy who got caught by his mom with his hand in the cookie jar.

**Mary-Ellen:**  Did you get more notes after that day?

**M&M:**  Oh, yeah...a-lot.  At first, one per week would be put in my locker—dropped in through the horizontal vents.  After I created and taped a cute mailbox sign on the outside and a shoe box on the inside of my locker to catch the notes, the number of notes increased to…more like four a week. Some weeks there was a note, poem or letter every morning.

**Mary-Ellen:** Was it creepy getting stuff every day? Did you think someone was stalking you? Were the notes inappropriate or suggestive?

**M&M:** Oh, no, not at all. They were mostly beautiful poems. Sweet, kind and tender words. Never anything inappropriate—not to me. Always signed "Yours, Anonymous."

**Mary-Ellen:** Have you saved the notes? Did you bring some with you today? Are you willing to share them with me, or at least one that was a typical example of the sort of thing you were receiving?

**M&M:** Here's one…probably my favorite. I'll read it to you:

## <u>Beyond Touch</u>

If I could capture
All of what you are
In words
These words
Would take up too much space...
They would get in the way of discovery-
The revelation of the next smile;
Your head tilted ever so slightly
In acknowledgement;
The soft line of your cheek

As you pass me by unaware
That you have touched me
In a way that hands cannot measure...
Out of touch.

**Yours,
Anonymous**

**Mary-Ellen:** Do you have the original paper copy?
Could I see it?

**M&M:** Sure...here you go.

**Mary-Ellen:** Wow. That's nice. Did you, Brenda, and Trudy ever try to catch Ty in the act of sticking a note in your locker?

**M&M:** All the time. To no avail. Of course, it wasn't Ty at all.

**Mary-Ellen:** How did you find out?

**M&M:** Brenda told me it was Ashley White at lunch one day last year.

**Mary-Ellen:** Your friends have all told me the same story. They said Brenda told everyone at your lunch table on Friday, May 10. Is that day/date accurate?

**M&M:** I believe it is.

**Mary-Ellen:** What I want to know is *exactly* what Brenda told you. What was her proof that Ashley White wrote the notes?

**M&M:** Brenda told us she had come to school on May 10 to drop off a late research paper for science class. I think it was for Mr. Kalapick. She was there about fifteen minutes before homeroom. The halls were empty and dark. On her way back from the science hallway, she turned the corner to the junior-senior corridor. As she came around the corner she saw someone at my locker at the far end of the hallway. She quietly snuck up on him and hid around the next corner so she could see what he was doing without, herself, being seen. She saw Ashley White take a note out of his backpack and stick it in my locker.

Brenda said she leaned against a locker and made a noise by accident and Ashley got scared off.  He didn't see her though.  She waited for a minute or two and then went to my locker.  She said the note hadn't dropped into the inside properly.  She said a corner was still sticking out so she gave it a tug and pulled it out.  She read it, of course.

**Mary-Ellen:**  But she waited to tell you and show you the note for several hours.  She had it with her and kept quiet about it for nearly half a day. Why do you suppose she waited until lunch to show you and everyone else at your table?

**M&M:**  I don't know.  Maybe she was thinking about exactly *how* to tell me.

**Mary-Ellen:**  Is it possible she waited for the right moment to do some "show and tell" in order to make a big deal out of it?  Do you think she may have  been trying to "play things up" to embarrass you and Ty?.

**M&M:**  Seams that way, doesn't it?

**Mary-Ellen:**  Yes, it does.  OK.  Now, at lunch that day did she point out Ashley sitting at a table across the room?  Did she make any comments about him?

**M&M:**  She did.  After she got Ty to admit he had a crush on me, she cracked up laughing and revealed the truth.  She pointed Ashley out and called him a "creepy stalker", "gross", etc.  She even physically shivered with disgust.  She went on and on, suggesting Ashley had been secretly creeping on me for months.  She really did a good job making Ashley seem disgusting in a dangerous way.

I told her to knock it off, but she obviously was enjoying the whole scene she had created.

**Mary-Ellen:**  How did Ty, Duwain and Marty react to what Brenda said and did?

**M&M:**  Ty was embarrassed into admitting he liked me…as more than a friend.  He got really quiet. Duwain and Marty started joking around and acting all tough, like, "We're going to teach this sick-freak for messing with our girl".  Brenda egged them on.  I don't remember Trudy saying anything, but she did laugh at the stuff the guys were saying. By the end of the lunch period Marty was talking about what they— the guys—were going to do to "teach Ashley a lesson".

**Mary-Ellen:**  Do you remember anything specifically about what Marty meant by "teaching Ashley a lesson?"

**M&M:**  Marty and Duwain said they were going to pull Ashley into the bathroom and give him a "Mexican swirly".

**Mary-Ellen:** What the heck is a "Mexican swirly"?

**M&M:**  They said it's when one of them "takes a dump" in a toilet.  Then they grab Ashley, hold him upside-down with his hands behind his back, and drop him head-first into the bowl.  Oh, and then flush it— hence, a "swirly".

**Mary-Ellen:** Oh, my God.  Were they serious?

**M&M:** Definitely.  They were laughing but they were completely serious about doing it—that afternoon.

**Mary-Ellen:** Did you encourage them?

**M&M:** No way.  Ashley didn't deserve that.  He didn't deserve anything close to that.  He was sweet and innocent.  They were just being jerks.  Total Neanderthals.  I told them to stop talking that way and I told them NOT to do ANYTHING to Ashley.

**Mary-Ellen:** Did they listen to you?

**M&M:** Yes.  But Marty made some snide remark about having "another, far superior plan" and bragged about doing something to send a clear message to Ashley to stop "sexually harassing" me.  Marty said his "Plan B" was "more subtle".  He said it was something nobody would get caught doing because nobody would be able to prove who did it to Ashley.

**Mary-Ellen:** Did you speak up when Marty said Ashley was sexually harassing you?

**M&M:** Yeah, but they all pretty much ignored my protest.  Again, I told them to forget about it, and to *stay away* from Ashley.

**Mary-Ellen:** So you're sure you told them to stay away from Ashley?

**M&M:** Yes.  I said it very angrily and firmly.  But Marty and Duwain laughed it off.  They did drop the subject totally though, so I honestly thought it was over.

**Mary-Ellen:**  Did you attend the party at Marty's house on Saturday that week?  If you did, tell me everything about it— especially anything about drug use.  I'll be upfront with you.  Your friends say you did X at that party.

**M&M:**  I'm embarrassed to admit it.  I did take one pill that night.  Never again, that's for sure.  It scared me.  I felt totally out of control, and I don't like that feeling.  Marty offered me a second pill later that night when Trudy and Brenda and I were going to watch a movie in his basement, but I flushed it down the toilet as soon as Marty went outside with Duwain and Ty.

**Mary-Ellen:**  Did Trudy and Brenda take X from Marty at that time?

**M&M:**  Yes.  Trudy knew better, but she got pressured by Brenda into taking it anyway, even after I begged her to flush it.  I didn't bother trying to convince Brenda.  She wouldn't listen to me anyway.

**Mary-Ellen:**  Some have said Mercedes Perez was dealing the X at Marty's party, and that Brent and Earl were the source.  Is this true; or are those people lying?

**M&M:**  Straight up liars.  I don't remember seeing Mercedes at the party, later.  She may have been there until around 9:00 when Brent and Earl went home.  People drank beer earlier, but I know for a fact that no X was being distributed or consumed until after the concert—after midnight or even later.  Mercedes was long gone.

**Mary-Ellen:** OK. About the X, as it relates to Ashley's death. The drug ecstasy was found in his blood work by the coroner. Either Ashley took X or someone slipped it into his drink at lunch on Monday the 13th. You were at the table with Marty, Duwain, Ty, Brenda and Trudy. Did you see any one among them leave your table and go over to Ashley's table while he was away from his table?

**M&M:** No. But I really wasn't paying attention to Ashley or his table.

**Mary-Ellen:** Some say Marty left the table and went to the lav, toward the end of the period. These same people told me Marty didn't return to your lunch table, but went directly to Ms. Lehrer's classroom. They say it was 10 minutes before the period ended. Is that accurate, as far as you know?

**M&M:** He did leave. That's true. But I don't remember where he went. I certainly didn't know, at the time, he was really going to Ms. Lehrer's classroom.

**Mary-Ellen:** Did he, by any chance, walk past Ashley's table on his way to the restroom?

**M&M:** Yes. He would have to walk the door directly between Ashley's table and the lunch line entrance door, if he were exiting to go to the bathroom. Like I said thought, I didn't watch him carefully. I had no idea he was up to anything.

**Mary-Ellen:** Did he put anything on Ashley's table while Ashley and Paisley were taking their lunch trays up?

**M&M:**  I told you, I don't know.  It's possible, I guess.

**Mary-Ellen:**  Do you know that a chocolate milk carton was left on Ashley's table while he and Paisley were away from their table?

**M&M:**  Yes, I've heard.

**Mary-Ellen:**  Have you heard that a yellow sticky note was affixed to this carton with a handwritten message from *you* on it?  This message said *you* appreciated the poems and that *you* sent him the chocolate milk to say thanks.

**M&M:**  I've heard, yes.

**Mary-Ellen:**  Well, did you write the message?  Did you or one of your friends place it on Ashley's table while he and Paisley were temporarily away?

**M&M:**  Oh, my…*no, no, no.*  I wouldn't do anything to Ashley.  I wouldn't lie to him.  And if I wanted to say thanks, I would have walked right up to him and said thanks.

**Mary-Ellen:**  So, you swear you didn't write the message or have the idea to give Ashley chocolate milk?

**M&M:**  I swear to God…Dear Jesus, no, I didn't send him anything.

**Mary-Ellen:**  Then tell me, who did?  Who used you to trick Ashley into drinking chocolate milk with X in it? He trusted you. He only drank the stuff because he was smitten with you and believed you had sent it.

**M&M:** I...don't know. I suspect Marty and Brenda... but I have no way to prove it.

**Mr. Flory:** Here's a tissue, M&M.

**Mary-Ellen:** OK. I know you're upset. I didn't intend to seem mean, but he *died*. I mean, this drug may have put him in such a confused state that he became suicidal.

**M&M:** Don't you think I know this? It tears me up inside! Look, I'm tired. We've been at this for 2 hours. I'm done. I can't believe you think I had anything to do with this X in the chocolate milk. I had no idea what Marty was planning to do to Ashley. I didn't know he, or anyone else, had drugged him. I didn't think Ashley was a "creepy stalker" like Brenda and Marty did. Everyone—other than those two—will tell you that I told them NOT to hurt or embarrass Ashley.

## Commentary on M&M's First Interview

There's no doubt in my mind that M&M was delighted to receive the anonymous flowers, notes, and poems. She never regarded these anonymous deliveries as inappropriate or suggestive. Over a period of two months, these romantic notes kept coming, and she never once reacted to them in such a way as to lead her friends to believe she was uncomfortable or "creeped out" by them. Nor did she ever express the notion that she was being "sexually harassed". M&M enjoyed getting this attention, even going so far as to encourage more attention by putting up a welcoming mail box sign on her locker.

The wide-spread notion among M&M's friends that these notes were being written by Ty Weiser was a major factor her happiness. She obviously *wanted* it to be Ty. After all, she never stopped to question what her friends were promoting. The unknown aspect created an aura of romanticism.

If M&M had known Ashley was the mystery author, I suspect she wouldn't have encouraged him to keep it up. She probably would have let him know that she knew he was writing the notes. She probably would have told him she appreciated the sentiment, but she wasn't interested in a relationship. Ashley probably would have been embarrassed. M&M doesn't seem like the type who would have publicly embarrassed Ashley though. Most likely, it would have ended there.

I find no reason to believe M&M would have regarded Ashley as a potentially dangerous, creepy stalker. That narrative was created and promoted by Brenda and Marty. Of course, the others—Duwain, Ty, and Trudy—went along with it.

M&M simply had no reason to be involved in spiking Ashley's chocolate milk. She didn't want to publicly embarrass him or get him kicked out of school. I believe the yellow sticky note attached to the carton was not her doing. She was the only person in that group who consistently told Marty and Duwain and Ty to leave Ashley alone. M&M's recollection of Marty and Duwain's original plan to give Ashley a "Mexican swirly" rings true. It is the sort of "prank" that others have told me Marty was fond of. M&M was horrified with the idea and clearly told them *not* to do it, or anything else.

M&M was at the lunch table with her friends the day of the "practical joke", but she didn't set up, run interference for, or participate in any element of Marty's plan.

I believe she told me the truth about the distribution and use of X at Marty's party. What she told me about her personal use and experience with the drug, and Trudy's giving in to Brenda's pressure to do more, fits circumstances and what I've come to know about Brenda's personality. Even more importantly, that M&M stated Marty was the source for the X, rather than Mercedes, confirms what Earl and Brent told me.

As far as figuring out who delivered the X-laced chocolate milk and "thank you" note, M&M's limited recollection was helpful. Only she, Brenda and Marty—not Mercedes—could have been in possession of X at the time. My gut tells me to eliminate M&M from this list. However, there is a chance she lied about flushing the X down the toilet at Marty's party, to cover for her saving it for future use.

As to who had the opportunity to deliver the carton to Ashley's table while he and Paisley were temporarily gone, putting their lunch trays away, it comes down to the same three.

Since my interview with M&M went sour before I had a chance to ask all the questions I intended to, I'm hoping she will consent to a second interview.

## Brenda Waxman

The following is the transcript of my interview with Brenda Waxman, conducted in the guidance office of Franklin High School, Jedesdorf, PA.

Date:  June 18, 2011
Time:  2:42-3:27 PM
Witness:  Mr. Roger D. Flory (Teacher).


**Mary-Ellen:**  Brenda, tell me a little something about yourself.

**Brenda:**  I'm 18 years old.  I'm a senior at Franklin. I've been a varsity cheerleader for 3 years.  I was captain of the squad during my junior year.  Um…

**Mary-Ellen:**  Who is your boyfriend?

**Brenda:** Marty Fine.

**Mary-Ellen:**  Are you going to college in the fall?

**Brenda:**  I plan to study fashion & design at F.I.T. (Fashion Institute of Technology) in New York City.

**Mary-Ellen:**  I've heard from others that you are a model.  Is that true?

**Brenda:**  I attend a local modeling school and I've been signed to a modeling agency in Manhattan.

**Mary-Ellen:** When I spoke with Mercedes Perez about you, she didn't have one kind word to say about you. Is the feeling mutual?

**Brenda:** I don't like Mercedes. She's a poser and wannabe. She should go back to Philly.

**Mary-Ellen:** Marty and others don't seem to have a problem with Mercedes. For example, everyone says that she was invited by Marty to his biggest party last May.

**Brenda:** Yeah, she was invited to Marty's party…by Marty. That was because one of the guys in Marty's band was [verb censored] that. Oh, and Trudy and Mercedes were friends at the time. I doubt they are now. Marty didn't hang around her. She's a thug. She was doing and giving people X. She even gave some to Marty and Marty may have tried it, but he's not a druggie, he just made a mistake.

**Mary-Ellen:** Let's move on to another important subject: the secret admirer notes and poems. Did you think the notes M&M were receiving anonymously were being sent by Ty Weiser?

**Brenda:** I thought it was funny when the secret admirer turned out to be Ashley White because I thought the handwritten notes looked a lot like Ty Weiser's handwriting. I compared the handwritten ones to Ty's English notebook. It looked like a match to me.

**Mary-Ellen:** You're not a graphologist or a professional document examiner, are you?

**Brenda:** What a stupid question.  Of course, I'm not. People compare handwriting all the time.  I never said I was a professional [expletive deleted].

**Mary-Ellen:** Take it easy.  No offense was intended.

**Brenda:** Next question. Let's keep this moving.

**Mary-Ellen:** Did you play up the Ty Weiser angle?  If so, what was your motive?  The way others tell what you did and said on Friday, May 10, at lunch, it sounds like you were trying to cause an overreaction or stir up anger against Ashley.

**Brenda:** I'm not sure what you mean.  But, if you are asking me whether I teased M&M and Ty about the whole thing…well, sure.  It was just a bit of fun to get them to 'fess up to their mutual 'secret' infatuation. Sure, I teased M&M and Ty about the notes at lunch. But I did it to get Ty to admit that he liked M&M— nothing more.  Ty *did* admit to liking M&M.

**Mary-Ellen:** Did the guys at your table get angry with Ashley White once you revealed he was the "Yours, Anonymous"?

**Brenda:** Yes.  Ty and Duwain were especially pissed. I don't remember the guys talking about getting even with Ashley for being a stalker.

**Mary-Ellen:** Stalker?  Did the guys call Ashley a stalker?

**Brenda:**  Yes, after I pointed him out Ty and Duwain called Ashley a stalker.  They didn't talk about teaching Ashley as lesson or anything nasty though.

**Mary-Ellen:**  You know…I'm puzzled by your choice of words.  I *never* asked about whether they called Ashley a stalker.  *You* took it upon *yourself* to introduce the word.  Is that because you are trying to cast the blame on *them* for calling Ashley a stalker when it was actually *you* who were first to suggest Ashley was a "creepy stalker?"  After all, *everyone* else told me those were *your* words…not Ty's or Duwain's.

**Brenda:**  Whoever said that is a *liar* trying to cover their [expletive deleted].

**Mary-Ellen:**  Moving on…Tell me about what you witnessed on the morning of May 10, before the start of the school day.

**Brenda:**  I saw Ashley sneaking around M&M's locker.  It seemed menacing, like he was a stalker or something weird.  He had written SO MANY of these creepy romantic notes.  No normal person would write so many anonymous love notes!  It's like that's how he got his sick jollies.

**Mary-Ellen:**  But you thought it had been Ty.  Right?

**Brenda:**  Yeah…so?

**Mary-Ellen:**  So…you never accused Ty of stalking M&M all those months when you say you were convinced it was him.

**Brenda:** For obvious reasons. Ty's not creepy. He's not a stalker. We wouldn't mind *him* being secretive. He's our friend. He's a hottie. As for Ashley…he's none of those things. Besides, he followed me and M&M around in the hallways. He was stalking us for months.

**Mary-Ellen:** OK, enough about that. Paisley Wahr told me a chocolate milk carton was delivered by some unknown person to their lunch table on the day in question. What do you know about this?

**Brenda:** Mercedes Perez wrote the note to Ashley White and gave him the chocolate milk, pretending it was M&M. Mercedes sits at the next table over from Ashley and Paisley. I have heard it was spiked with X. Mercedes is a dealer. She obviously did it.

**Mary-Ellen:** Are you saying that you *saw* Mercedes put the chocolate milk on Ashley's table?

**Brenda:** I didn't know why she was doing it, but yes I saw her put the carton down on the table as she walked passed to get in line to put away her tray. Ashley and Paisley went to take their trays up. While they were away and nobody else was at their table, Mercedes stood up and walked over. She pretended to drop the chocolate milk on the floor, so she could pick it up and place it on table at Ashley's place. You can't trust Mercedes. She's a criminal and a bully.

**Mary-Ellen:** If what you are saying is true, why didn't a single person at Mercedes' table see what she did? I have talked to every member of the softball team. Not a single girl remembers what you are describing.

**Brenda:** She sits close to Ashley White at lunch. They probably missed it. Mercedes is a sneaky [expletive deleted].

**Mary-Ellen:** Where was Marty at the time you say Mercedes was "being sneaky?"

**Brenda:** He was sitting right next to me at our table.

**Mary-Ellen:** Oh, really? So you're saying he didn't leave the table during the last 10 minutes of the lunch period to put away his tray early and then use the restroom.

**Brenda:** That's right, Sherlock. He had a packed lunch, so he didn't even have a tray.

**Mary-Ellen:** After lunch, you went to Ms. Lehrer's class; correct?

**Brenda:** Yes.

**Mary-Ellen:** You and Trudy distracted Ms. Lehrer on purpose so Marty, Ty and Duwain could set up their prank on Ashley.  Right?

**Brenda:** No, NOT right.  I was talking with her in the hallway, but I didn't know what Ty and Duwain were up to inside.  Marty, as far as I know, was still in the restroom.

**Mary-Ellen:** Wait a minute.  Didn't you just say that Marty *didn't* go to the restroom at the end of the period?

**Brenda:**  He went between periods and came in late to Ms. Lehrer's class just before Ashley went ballistic, freaked out, bolted across the room and fell off the chair.

**Mary-Ellen:**  Can you explain why nobody else in that class, including the teacher, remembers Marty coming to class late?

**Brenda:**  I-dunno.  Like usual, they're all oblivious. Ms. Lehrer was taking attendance on her laptop and talking with Trudy.  By that time Ty and Duwain had unscrewed the chair Ashley fell from, so they're just attempting to escape any blame if they told you a different story.

**Mary-Ellen:**  I've interviewed other people who were in the classroom when Ashley got hurt. Everyone, with the exception of your boyfriend, says you were laughing about Ashley getting hurt.  They say he was out cold and some thought he might even be dead, but you were laughing your head off and even texting people in other classes.

**Brenda:**  They're liars.  They're all covering for themselves.

**Mary-Ellen:**  Really?

**Brenda:**  REALLY.  *They* were all laughing at Ashley.  I laughed a little, until I could see he might be hurt. Others, like Duwain and Ty, kept laughing and laughing.

**Mary-Ellen:** Yet, *you* had the presence of mind to text people about what happened—joking about it. You're the *only one* who did *that*. Others could have, but they didn't. I've seen the texts because it went viral, so don't deny it. Here, take a look. "AW" is obviously Ashley White. You wrote, "creepr dwn justice servd ROFL"

**Brenda:** Yeah. What about it? I text all the time. It's a bit of an obsession.

**Mary-Ellen:** In this text, what did you mean by "creepr dwn"?

**Brenda:** Creeper down.

**Mary-Ellen:** It seems like you are admitting a motive here with these words. To me, you are saying that a prank was perpetrated on Ashley because you thought he was creeping on M&M.

**Brenda:** No. I just thought he was a creepy guy. He was. That doesn't mean I knew about the prank Ty and Duwain did.

**Mary-Ellen:** I think I've heard *enough*. You can go. *Just leave.*

**Brenda:** What's your problem? Don't be a jerk, just because the *truth* doesn't match your agenda…little miss know-it-all. Give it up. You're embarrassing yourself. You're a pathetic loser. I knew I shouldn't have agreed to this stupid interview.

## Commentary on Brenda Waxman's Interview

Brenda was everything I expected she'd be. I'm going to refrain from writing too much about this shallow jerk, because that would be prejudicial. I tried my best not to dislike her. I failed.

If instincts mean anything in an investigation, mine told me to distrust just about everything she said. It seemed like her every response was intended to avoid telling the truth. She tried to blame everyone else for what happened, except for Marty, of course.

Perhaps her only truthful answers involved her descriptions of how she felt about the people she considers beneath her.

Ashley was one of those whom she regarded as beneath her. The way she reacted to seeing him at M&M's locker is crucial in this respect.

Perhaps "reacted" is not the best way to describe her response to her discovery that Ashley was M&M's secret admirer. I say this because the word "reacted" doesn't adequately describe what actions Brenda took. After all, Brenda didn't immediately tell M&M and her other friends what she had seen. Rather, she took her time and thought about how she could best use this juicy discovery. Then she played it up with the use of a type of exaggeration intended to create an atmosphere of intolerance toward Ashley from her friends. It was even more than that. She laid the necessary groundwork for her friends to draw irrational and hateful conclusions by creating an extremely awkward situation.

How so? Well, it's clear to me that she purposefully tried to embarrass Ty and M&M by initially claiming Ty was the source of all the love notes. She emotionally manipulated all of her friends at that lunch table with this blatant lie. She succeeded in toying with their emotional vulnerability. Ty even buckled under this pressure and admitted he had a crush on M&M.

What's the big deal with some harmless teasing designed to get a friend to tell the truth? Not much, unless you consider Brenda clearly used this emotionally charged moment to provoke the guys into a potentially hurtful overreaction. She, in fact, intended to provoke this reaction from the guys by suddenly turning everyone's attention to Ashley.

Even though she didn't know Ashley, and had never once really seen him following M&M around, she intentionally misled her friends by mischaracterizing him as a danger to M&M. She did a fine acting job, convincing her friends. Everyone present at that lunch table recalls just how freaked out Brenda was when she revealed "creepy stalker".

Finally, some might object to my suggestion that Brenda was *acting*, because it's possible Brenda just looking at Ashley White made her skin crawl. To her, Ashley was clearly beneath her and her friends. In Brenda's mind, she probably thought "putting him in his place" was necessary.

I acknowledge this objection of Brenda's mind-set but I also assert she also purposely acted in such a way as to make her natural reaction even more pronounced than it actually was. This extra effort was designed to ramp up the guys.

Brenda certainly wouldn't have acted the same way if she'd witnessed a stranger who she deemed "a hottie" attempting to deliver love notes to M&M. She may have used this to get Ty to admit he liked M&M, but nobody in their right mind would believe she would have described the "hottie" as a dangerous, creepy stalker.

Of course, in my interview with her, Brenda placed blame on Duwain and Ty for the prejudicial description of Ashley. Do I believe her? Absolutely not.

# Trudy Schroeder

The following is the transcript of my interview with Trudy Schroeder, conducted in the guidance office of Franklin High School, Jedesdorf, PA.

Date: June 19, 2011
Time: 2:40-3:21 PM
Witness: Mr. Roger D. Flory (Teacher).


**Mary-Ellen:** Trudy, tell me about the extra-curricular activities you're involved in.

**Trudy:** I'm a varsity cheerleader in the fall only. I play softball in the spring with my friend, Mercedes. She plays second base and I play third.

**Mary-Ellen:** Are you involved in any in-school activities beyond your regular classes?

**Trudy:** I co-anchor the morning school news program with Marty Fine.

**Mary-Ellen:** That's interesting. Do you want to be a news anchor someday?

**Trudy:** Yes, I do.

**Mary-Ellen:** That's interesting. Let's put that aside for now and come back to it later.

I have a really important question. Would you tell me about what happened at your lunch table on Friday,

May 10?  Specifically, tell me as much as you can remember about what Brenda said and did.

**Trudy:**  I was at the lunch table on Friday, May 10 when Brenda threw the secret admirer note onto Ty's lunch tray.  Ty was surprised and denied any involvement.  Then Brenda pointed to the opposite side of the cafeteria at Ashley White and told us it was him who had been doing it the whole time.  Brenda called Ashley a creepy stalker.  M&M protested and told Brenda to shut up.  Brenda didn't shut up and kept teasing Ty and M&M.  Brenda actually got Ty to admit that he liked M&M.  Then the guys started joking about what they used to do to nerds and geeks in class back in 8th grade.  We had no idea what they were laughing about, but Duwain and Marty said they would "teach the stalker a lesson."  Again M&M intervened and told them to knock it off.  She warned them not to dare lay a finger on Ashley.

Things got pretty intense, but the guys left us under the impression it was all just a silly joke and they weren't going to do anything.  But Marty came to me on the morning of Monday, May 13, and asked me to "Keep Ms. Lehrer out in the hallway at the beginning of 6th period."  He said he was going to steal the answer key to her final exam because he knew where she kept it in her desk. I had no idea Marty and the other guys were really up to something else.  I had no idea what they were going to do.  I had no idea they were planning to hurt Ashley.

With Brenda, I kept Ms. Lehrer out in the hallway until Duwain gave me the all clear sign.

**Mary-Ellen:**  Didn't you hear about the plan to embarrass Ashley White at Marty's party?

**Trudy:** No.  Marty never said any such thing at his party...at least not around me.

**Mary-Ellen:** Did it seem strange that Marty would ask you to distract Ms. Lehrer?  Or had he used you or others to help him steal before?

**Trudy:** Um...Well, stealing answer keys is something I knew he did before.  He hadn't asked me to help out before.

**Mary-Ellen:** Did you guys ever get together with a cheat-sheet...later?

**Trudy:** No. I don't believe Marty stole Ms. Lehrer's answer key on Monday.  He obviously lied to me to get me to participate in something I might otherwise object to.

**Mary-Ellen:** Ok, let's switch gears.
I want to read a letter to you that Mr. Denker shared with me.  He had called you into his office to talk about it and then he spoke with your parents about it.  Your mom gave me a copy, otherwise Mr. Denker would not have shared it with me.  Apparently, Mr. Denker was forced to share it with the police and the District Attorney.  He wanted to keep it in confidence, but was overruled by the DA.


Mr. D,
    It seems a little weird to use this *questions box thing* to ask you a question, but I can't just walk into your office.

This past year me and my friends have been taking these pills called "rolls." They come in many different varieties, such as "Green CK's," "Pink Panthers," "Buddas". They have a little picture on them that goes along with the name. Most of my friends haven't even heard of them before and I was just wondering if you had. I was also wondering if you could tell me what is in them. They make your vision jump around and your sense of touch really intense. You're numb until you touch something or something touches you, then you can feel it through your entire body. And I always tell people how much I love them, even if I don't like the person.

Everyone thinks these pills are harmless and I feel like I could stop at any time. Still, you told me I could talk to you about any problems and that you'd keep it confidential. Could I come down to see you this afternoon?

Trudy S.

**Mary-Ellen:** Please explain what your note means.

**Trudy:** I never sent any note to Mr. Denker. I never experimented with ecstasy and have no idea whether any of my other friends used any drugs. I've never seen them use drugs.

**Mary-Ellen:** Do you deny sending the letter? Do you deny putting this letter in the guidance office Questions and Concerns Box? I talked to your parents. *They* believe you wrote it.

**Trudy:** Yes they do, but I didn't write it. Even if my friends were doing drugs, I'm no snitch. Plus, Mr. Denker is creepy. I would never go to his office alone.

**Mary-Ellen:** Duwain told me you'd say something like that about Mr. Denker.

**Trudy:** Duwain was right. He knows me.

**Mary-Ellen:** He's your boyfriend. Right?

**Trudy:** Yes.

**Mary-Ellen:** Back to Mr. Denker.
   If Mr. Denker was behaving inappropriately towards you and other girls, why the heck didn't you report him?

**Trudy:** He's never actually touched anyone or anything like that. It's just the way he looks at me…and other pretty girls. I don't want to wreck his marriage or anything, just because he obviously appreciates pretty girls.

**Mary-Ellen:** OK…wait, how do you know whether Mr. Denker is married or not?

**Trudy:** I-donno. A few of the girls used to think he was cute. They didn't know he was married until they noticed some pics on his desk…or something like that. I don't remember who told me.

**Mary-Ellen:** Be honest about those girls. Where some of them flirting with Mr. Denker *before* they figured out he was married?

**Trudy:** Maybe *they* did...but not *me*.

**Mary-Ellen:** Did it ever cross your mind that Mr. Denker acted a bit strange around you girls after you girls started acting strange around him?

**Trudy:** That's no excuse to flirt with teenage girls.

**Mary-Ellen:** Are you one-hundred percent sure he was flirting? Could he have just been acting in an awkward way because these girls had flirted with him?

**Trudy:** I-donno. Maybe it was something like that. He made me feel uncomfortable. What more do you want me to say?

**Mary-Ellen:** Moving on then...Why did you laugh at Ashley when he jumped on the chair and it collapsed in Ms. Lehrer's class?

**Trudy:** I didn't laugh at Ashley when he fell off the chair and hurt himself. I was scared he might be dead. He didn't move for like two minutes.

After Ashley woke up he acted like a psycho. He went crazy and stormed out of the classroom. He couldn't be consoled by anyone—not by the teacher or the nurse. I remember him swearing at me and Marty and Ty and Brenda, saying he was "leaving and never coming back." Brenda was the only one laughing at him. Just because she was looking at me and laughing doesn't mean that I was laughing.

**Mary-Ellen:** Other students in Ms. Lehrer's class told me you were laughing with Brenda.

**Trudy:** Whoever said that is a liar. Tell me, who told you?

**Mary-Ellen:** That's confidential.

**Trudy:** Well, then this 'interview', or should I say interrogation, is over.

[Trudy picked up her belongings and stomped out of the room, muttering something unintelligible]

## Commentary on Trudy Schroeder's Interview

Trudy is in total denial about her willing role in the prank that led to Ashley's death.  It seems possible to she may not have known exactly what had been planned or what was going on in Ms. Lehrer's classroom.

She does seem to have a conscious. On the other hand, she definitely lacks the willpower to put it into action. Even if she had known the specifics of what was being planned, and how dangerous it potentially was, I'm still convinced she would have remained mute about it.

I think it is entirely possible Trudy was present when at Marty's party he shared the details of the vicious prank he was intending to pull off. Trudy, who, according to M&M, was high on X at the time, probably doesn't remember a thing.  In similar fashion, her claim that Marty told her a lie about stealing Ms. Lehrer's answer key is believable.  She was deceived into being an unwitting accessory to the crime.

Did she laugh along with Brenda, as Ashley lay unconscious on the floor in Ms. Lehrer's room? Probably.

Did she have a conscious enough about the possible danger of the drug ecstasy to her and her friends that she wrote a letter to the guidance counselor?  Yes. Again, she lacked the willpower to follow through. There's no evidence to support my theory on this one, but I can imagine Brenda or Duwain, or both, somehow found out about it and came up with the whole story of Mr. Denker hitting on "pretty girls" in order to create a big distraction from the contents of the letter.

## Mercedes Perez

The following is the transcript of my interview with Mercedes Perez, conducted in the guidance office of Franklin High School, Jedesdorf, PA.

Date: June 20, 2011
Time: 2:40-3:22 PM
Witness: Mr. Roger D. Flory (Teacher).

**Mary-Ellen:** Everyone has told me you and your family moved here from Philly. Is that correct?

**Mercedes:** They're correct. I haven't attended Franklin all my life like most people here. I lived and went to school in Philadelphia until the beginning of my junior year.

**Mary-Ellen:** I heard from one of your teachers that you're a budding writer. Ashley White loved writing too.

**Mercedes:** I'd like to think that's true. I love to write and want to be an author some day. I've been working on a novel. I really only knew Ashley White because he was in my creative writing class during our junior year. He was, by far, the best writer in the school.

**Mary-Ellen:** Were you jealous of his writing ability?

**Mercedes:** What?

**Mary-Ellen:** It's a simple question.

**Mercedes:** Of course I wasn't jealous of his creative writing abilities. Why would you even ask such a question?

**Mary-Ellen:** Well, at least two people I've spoken with about Ashley seem to think you had some sort of reason to embarrass him by spiking his chocolate milk with ecstasy. One person told me they saw you put a carton at Ashley's table at lunch on Monday, May 13. And Ashley's best friend said this carton had a note on it from M&M.

**Mercedes:** Did Paisley say *I* did that? Did she say I was jealous of Ashley? Why would she say that? She knows that's not true. It was Marty.

**Mary-Ellen:** No. The part I mentioned about Paisley is about what she saw when she returned to the lunch table that Monday. She and Ashley had taken their lunch trays up. When they returned to their table, there was a carton of chocolate milk with a note on it which Ashley believed came from M&M. Someone else said they saw you put the carton there.

**Mercedes:** Trudy's my best friend. She wouldn't lie about me. It sounds more like Brenda. It was Brenda, wasn't it?

**Mary-Ellen:** I want to ask a question before we talk about Brenda...

**Mercedes:** No, I've got to say something about this false accusation. In the interest of full disclosure, I admit it...I can't stand her. She's a stuck up jerk who enjoys hurting other people.  She gets her kicks by provoking people, getting people to hate each other, and picking on people she thinks are inferior to her. That's the truth.  Anyone who says different is either scared of her, her boyfriend Marty, or owes her something.

**Mary-Ellen:**  OK.  Then explain to me why the heck Trudy has anything to do with her.  If Brenda is as evil as you portray her, why would your best friend hang around her and Marty all the time?  Trudy is a close friend of yours.  Surely you've confronted her about Brenda.

**Mercedes:**  I've been trying to convince Trudy to stop hanging around Marty and Brenda for a long time. Marty is a drug dealer, but he's too clever to get caught. I hate to admit it, but Marty and Brenda are very smart. That doesn't make them good people, though.  The word that comes to mind is "evil".  I don't eat lunch with Duwain or Trudy because of Brenda and Marty. All Brenda ever did, the few times I ate lunch with them last year, was make fun of my clothes, car and accent and everyone else in the school that didn't meet her twisted standards.  She is the most materialistic person I've ever met.  That's probably why she's Marty's girlfriend.  He's the son of the richest dad in the school district.  Supposedly he's an executive for a high profile chemical engineering corporation.  But I know Marty isn't dealing ecstasy and getting away with it by accident.  Marty's dad has some shady connections to foreign chem labs.  That's where the big money comes from.  One time Marty was high after a basketball game and he started telling me, Trudy and Ty about his dad's connections to drugs and diamonds in Amsterdam.  Actually, Marty bragged about it several times.

For example, Marty's parents were in the Netherlands at the time of the infamous party last year. They had full knowledge of their son's dealing and even bought the beer for the party.  Because good old Daddy Fine has friends on the police force, they never bust his punk kid's parties.  If I had those sort of parties at my house, I'd be in juvee *right now*.

**Mary-Ellen:**  Let's get back to Ashley.  Tell me what you know about his crush on M&M and the anonymous love notes.

**Mercedes:**  I had no idea Ashley White was writing love notes to Mary Margaret.  I assumed Ty Weiser wrote the notes because that's what Trudy and Brenda always said to me.

**Mary-Ellen:**  Tell me more about exactly what Brenda said to you about M&M and Ty.

**Mercedes:**  Well, one time Brenda said Ty and M&M were "secretly shacking up".  She said it was all hush-hush because Coach Dolce would "kill" Ty if he "found out".  I refused to repeat the rumor.  Brenda was obviously trying to spread a lie.

**Mary-Ellen:**  She said Coach Dolce would "kill" Ty?

**Mercedes:**  That's the word she used.  I assumed she meant that Coach Dolce would be really, really, angry. You know, "kill" doesn't always actually mean *kill*. People talk that way all the time and don't mean to be taken literally.

**Mary-Ellen:** Understood.

Something just came to mind.  I want to go back to what you saw at lunch on Monday, May 13.

**Mercedes:**  I was sitting at the next table over from Ashley and Paisley.  While they were away from their table I noticed Marty walk by their table and pick up something from off the floor. He placed it on the table and then walked away.  I wasn't sure if it was trash or what.

**Mary-Ellen:**  Did you see him drink the chocolate milk or reading a sticky note?

**Mercedes:**  No.  I wasn't paying attention to what Marty had placed on the table.

**Mary-Ellen:**  Are you sure?

**Mercedes:**  I'm sure.  I'd like to help you out here.  I believe Marty put chocolate milk on Ashley's table, but I'd be lying if I told you I knew for certain.  I didn't see exactly what it was.

**Mary-Ellen:**  What happened to Ashley in class after lunch?

**Mercedes:**  I was in another classroom when the prank went down in Ms. Lehrer's class.  Around 2:30 that afternoon I heard the roar of an engine in the parking lot and I looked out the classroom window to see Ashley peeling out in the parking lot and heading out at a great rate of speed.

**Mary-Ellen:** Let me show you a picture, just to be certain. Is this the car you saw speeding away from school?

**Mercedes:** That's definitely the one. That's Ashley's car. That's him in the picture after school one day. The boy standing next to him is Max. I don't know Max very well, but I know they were in the tuba section of the marching band together. They were close friends.

## Commentary on Mercedes Perez's Interview

What impressed me most about my interview of Mercedes was she could have lied about what she saw Marty doing when he walked by Ashley's lunch table on Monday, May 13.  It would have been a convenient way to get revenge on Marty and Brenda for telling outright lies about her, but she didn't.  They blamed her for delivering the ecstasy-laced chocolate milk, and she didn't return evil for evil.

That's why I believed her when she told me that there's no more fitting word to describe Marty and Brenda than evil.

As far as I can tell, Mercedes Perez had absolutely no reason to try to embarrass Ashley White by spiking his drink.  The notion she'd do that because she was jealous of Ashley's writing ability is silly and unbelievable.

# Group Interview

The following is the transcript of my group interview conducted in the guidance suite at Franklin High School, Jedesdorf, PA.

Five 8th grade girls participated in this roundtable session. Their names have been changed to protect their identities.

Date:  June 20, 2011
Time:  3:50-5:10 PM
Witnesses:  Dr. Lee Gallman (Principal) and Mr. Karl Denker (Guidance Counselor)


**Mary-Ellen:**  Dr. Gallman and Mr. Denker, I want to thank you for helping me organize this round table interview session.   I also want to thank everyone on the student panel for their participation today.  I don't know any of you guys, and that's the way it should be. The last thing I would want to do is to prejudice the process.

   Mr. Denker, would you explain to the student why they are here?

**Mr. Denker:**  Certainly.  Ms. Gerhard is a senior student at Franklin working on her graduation project. As eighth graders, you probably haven't had the pleasure of meeting Mary-Ellen, but she is a fine student.  More than that, she is a concerned citizen. You have been selected to be on this panel today because, likewise, you have a good reputation for honesty, reliability and good citizenship.  You are here today because you were selected as the five best-qualified students out of 50 recommended by your middle school teachers.

What Mary-Ellen needs from you today is your honest opinion about some poems written by a high school boy to a high school girl. This boy obviously had a serious crush on a senior girl—a very popular girl. This boy didn't ever come out and tell this girl about his feelings. Instead, this boy started writing this girl notes and poems in the hope that the girl would figure it out. He slipped many notes and poems into this girl's locker, over a period of a few months.

Students who know about these poems in the high school are divided about them. Some think they are innocent and even endearing. Others think they are creepy and have called the boy a stalker for writing anonymous notes and poems. This boy never attached his name to these items. He simply signed them "Yours, Anonymous."

Dr. Gallman, do you have anything you'd like to add?

**Dr. Gallman:** Yes. Please keep an open mind and don't feel intimidated by our presence (referring to himself and Mr. Denker). Tell Mary-Ellen what you think...and how you feel about the poems...whether they are sweet, scary, nice, or creepy, don't be afraid to say so. Mary-Ellen is looking for unbiased opinions.

Do you know what I mean?

[All 5 students nod yes]

**Dr. Gallman:** Great. Mary-Ellen...

**Mary-Ellen:** OK, guys, it's just like they said about the boy who wrote notes and poems to a girl who was a senior last year. The boy was crushing on her and writing her nearly every day. I want to share copies of these poems with you—just the ones that the high school students who knew about them disagree about...whether they were sweet or creepy.

Here's the first one. It's the first full poem this boy wrote to this girl. Read it silently. I'll give you a couple of minutes. Tell me how it makes you feel. Tell me, for instance, if you received this poem, how would you feel not knowing who it was from?

### <u>Beyond Touch</u>

If I could capture
All of what you are
In words
These words
Would take up too much space...
They would get in the way of discovery-
The revelation of the next smile;
Your head tilted ever so slightly
In acknowledgement;
The soft line of your check
As you pass me by unaware
That you have touched me
In a way that hands cannot measure...
Out of touch.
**Yours,**
**Anonymous**

**Mary-Ellen:** Have you guys had enough time?

[All five girls nod yes]

**Mary-Ellen:**  As girls, does this poem seem threatening or creepy to you in any way?

**Katie:**  Not creepy or scary or anything like that.  I would be really curious about who wrote this if some nameless person gave it to me.  It would probably drive me crazy trying to figure out who wrote it.
   Did she figure out who wrote it?

**Mary-Ellen:** Nope.  She had no idea.

**Lizzy:**  Katie's right, I wouldn't like not knowing.  It's only creepy in a mysterious way, not in a threatening way.  Well, creepy isn't the right word for it.  I'm not sure what to call it.

**Meghan:**  I hate secrets.  This poem isn't creepy but if I got it from some secret guy I'd be thinking about it a lot and trying to get my friends to help me figure out who it came from.

**Katie:**  Me too.  Did her friends help her figure it out?

**Mary-Ellen**:  Sort of.  Her friends thought it was a boy in their class that they all knew very well—a good looking, popular boy.  They didn't have any proof and the boy they thought it might be denied it right away.

**Dani:** If I thought it was from someone like that, it wouldn't be creepy to me.  It would probably make me happy to get a poem like that.

**Laura:**  I agree with Dani.  If some hot guy wrote that for me...I'd be smiling all day.

**Lizzy:** Some guys deny it when it's still them.

**Dani:** Yeah. How would she know that this guy wasn't just shy and stuff? Did this popular boy really like her?

**Mary-Ellen:** Yes he did. But he didn't write the poems. He was telling the truth.

**Lizzy:** So, who did; some other cute guy in her class?

**Mary-Ellen:** Someone in her class. That's all I'm going to say about the real writer at this point. I don't want you to think of him in any particular way before you read more of his anonymous poems.

   OK, so, in the part where this unknown guy says, "If I could capture all of what you are..."
Do you find that threatening? The word capture, is that a threat?

**Laura:** [Laughing] No. Really? It obviously doesn't mean that kind of "capture".

**Lizzy:** I agree.

[All five girls look at each other and express their agreement in various non-verbal ways]

**Mary-Ellen:** What about the part of the poem where he says,

> The soft line of your cheek
> As you pass me by unaware

That you have touched me...

**Mary-Ellen:** Does that sound like he's stalking the girl to you guys?

**Dani:** No.

**Meghan:** It sounds like he's going between classes and sees her and then goes and writes about it. It doesn't seem like he's hiding around the corner and spying on her or something. Besides, he's writing about how he thinks her face is pretty. If the guy was a creeper, he'd be writing her a poem about some other body part.

**Dani:** Meghan's right. Not sound weird or anything, but I imagine a creeper writing things about inappropriate parts...if you know what I mean.

**Laura:** I don't know. The more you talk about it possibly being stalking, the easier it is to start imagining it is stalking, even though it didn't seem weird at all at first.

**Mary-Ellen:** What do you mean, Laura. Explain what you're thinking.

**Laura:** Um...if I put myself in this girl's position, and if I kept getting all these poems—even if they all seemed innocent and sweet—after a while I might start to find weirdness.

**Katie:** Laura is right. It depends how long this kept up. Nobody likes a secret that never ends.

If this was a few months, maybe I'd start to feel it was a stalker thing. Mary-Ellen, did you ever talk with this girl and ask her if it got creepy for her right away or after a while?

**Mary-Ellen:** The girl told me that she never, ever found it creepy. Of course, she thought these notes came from someone she thought was hot.

**Katie:** That makes sense to me. What about her friends? After a few months, did they think it might be someone else?

**Mary-Ellen:** One of them did. We'll talk about that later. First, I want to share a few more samples with you.

Here's another. It's the last one he put in her locker. This way you'll see the first and last, back to back.

## A Tap on the Shoulder

It's fall again and the spirit calls out
Across the spot where I first saw you;
Around the bend of steps littered leafy-brown
A silent smile of acknowledgment still remains.

It's that time of year when my soul is played
Like a mourning oboe;
A tune that lifts me up on the pathway,
But which dashes me upon the same steps
Which my heart can never ascend.

The feel of fall...
So empty without you

(no falling in love).
The sailing leafs...
So purposeless without you.

Shall I go to that spot where your spirit haunts
And touch the stones over which you once tread?
Will I find one golden thread of your existence?
Oh, Lord ...
What I could have,
Would have,
Should have said!

I remember so well how
The words of your heart
Were like the leafs on the trees,
Falling from your eyes so silently...
Today, an oak-leaf gently came to rest upon my
shoulder
As I passed that spot.
And it, as if an extension of a past time, reminded me
of a day
When I should have been bolder.

**Yours,
Anonymous**

**Mary-Ellen:** That's a bit longer than the first.  Have you had enough time to think about it?

[All five girls respond with a subdued yes]

**Mary Ellen:** Meghan, you look like this one bothers you. What are you thinking?

**Meghan:** This is very different from the first. The first one was filled with hope. It was like he imagined he might have a chance, or at least one day have the guts to tell this girl to her face how he felt. In this one, he seems to have lost all hope. It's a bit depressing.

**Lizzy:** Yeah, it is. Like he may be giving up, or may have just given up.

**Mary-Ellen:** Is this creepy or does it seem to be something a stalker would write?

**Dani:** No way. This guy really loves her and it has him down...really down...knowing he'll never have a chance. I don't think the popular guy would have written this. The popular guys that I know have way too high self-esteem to write like that. They're usually the opposite—kinda cocky.

**Katie:** Yes, cocky. I don't know any who would write something like that. Not any 8th grade boys, that's for sure. They might write a poem if forced to do it in class, that's it.

**Lizzy:** [Laughing] Sooo true. Probably only about farts. How does that one go? "Here I sit all broken hearted..."

**Mary-Ellen:** [chuckling, trying to keep a straight face] So, would any of you guys feel threatened by this?

[All five girls (and the principal) are laughing. The girls shake their heads no].

**Mary-Ellen:** Enough. Let's get back to business. How about this one? He put it in her locker after writing her for about a month.

## Beyond the Shadow

Your beauty
Peels away the cold and silence
Like the kiss of a warm breeze
Greeting me in early spring
As an unexpected delight.

Your countenance,
Like the rising sun,
Chases away my imperfections
Hiding just beyond
The shadow of a doubt.

Yours,
Anonymous

**Mary-Ellen:** Ready?

[Everyone nods yes, except for Katie. Katie, looking out the window, seems to be a thousand miles away in her mind]

**Mary-Ellen:** Are you okay, Katie?

**Katie:** I'm sad for him.

**Lizzy:** Me too.

**Meghan:** Me three.

**Dani:** This isn't a love poem. It's like he's putting her up on a, uh, what's the word?

**Mary-Ellen:** Pedestal?

**Dani:** Yeah, that's it; pedestal.

**Katie:** If I were the girl getting these poems I think I would know after receiving this many poems that this guy is never gonna let me know who he is. I'd know he was afraid. Personally, I would probably put up a sign on my locker telling him not to be afraid and to just tell me who he is. I'd promise not to tell anyone else if he would just admit to it.

**Laura:** I'd do that too. Did she?

**Mary-Ellen:** No.

**Laura:** Why the heck not? It's the obvious thing to do if you really want to know.

**Dani:** Well, maybe she didn't want to know the truth. Maybe fiction was better. Maybe the fiction that it was that popular boy suited her, you know...with her friends and all.

**Katie:** I think Dani's right.

**Meghan:** Me too. She didn't want the truth. Was she getting a lot of attention from her friends because of these mysterious love letters?

**Mary-Ellen:** Very much, especially from her closest friends.  He friends kept reinforcing the idea that that cute guy was writing it.

**Lizzy:** But, that doesn't seem realistic.

**Mary-Ellen:** What do you mean?

**Lizzy:** Realistic.  You know, like we all agreed before.  There must be more to the story. Something's missing.  Did this girl also secretly like the cute guy?

**Mary-Ellen:** Yes.

**Lizzy:** I knew it! Why didn't she just go to the cute guy and ask him directly?  It's because she knew it wasn't him.  They probably had classes together and she knew it couldn't be him.

**Dani:** She wanted it to be him.

**Meghan:** She did. It sounds to me like she was using the attention to smoke the cute guy out.

**Mary-Ellen:** Meghan, do you mean that you think the girl getting the love notes was using the notes to get the cute guy to admit he liked her?

**Meghan:** Yes.  No doubt about it.

**Mary-Ellen:** You are very perceptive.  This girl admitted it.  She loved getting the love notes, the attention, and she hoped to use them as leverage to get the cute guy to admit he liked her. She knew he liked her.

**Dani:** Wait. Did she suspect that the guy leaving the love poems wasn't cute?

**Mary-Ellen:** She really didn't think about it that way until one day a close friend pointed out who the notes were really coming from.

**Laura:** She did what? How did she know?

**Mary-Ellen:** The other girl actually saw the secret admirer putting a poem in the slats of the locker. Later that day at lunch the friend pointed out the boy who was really doing it.

**Meghan:** OMG! What was her reaction? What did this guy look like? Did she know him?

**Mary-Ellen:** I don't know if I can tell you guys the answers to those questions now. When I finish my report, you can read all about it.

**Katie:** Please, can you just tell us if the guy creepy?

**Mary-Ellen:** That's not for me to judge.

**Katie:** Even if he wasn't the cutest guy, I'd give him a chance.

**Dani:** Me too.

**Laura:** How did this girl's friends react when the real guy was pointed out?

**Mary-Ellen:** Well, the girl who did the pointing out also called the anonymous guy with the crush a "creepy stalker," a "geek" and other stuff. I'm sure you can imagine how she said it. She tried to embarrass her friend in front of other friends. She was trying to knock the girl that had been getting so much attention down a peg or two.

**Meghan:** Some girls are like that; shallow jerks.

**Mary-Ellen:** Now, I'm going to give you all copies of the other poems he wrote anonymously. Take some time to read them over.

[All five girls got very quiet and read for about 20 minutes].

Here is the text of what they reviewed:

### <u>Unbend My Heart</u>

As I fold your hair
In the palm of my hand
Letting touch lead to touch
And tenderness command
All thoughts without bounds
All horizons without end
You reach into my heart
And my soul unbends.
My mind, a coil of concern,
Fraught with the world and its ways,
Is transported to other times and days
And unburdened by your return.

## Overcast

Once a teardrop falls
We may wipe it from our cheek
But it can never retreat.
For every one that trickles down
On the outside
Two reside
Within
As shadow and memory...
One the weight of experience
The other the substance of insight.
If there are no shadows on a cloudy day
Please will someone explain the inner shadow
Of an overcast heart?


## Whispers

The world turns
'round a single point
And if you could hear
The convergent sound of many paths
The mountains would speak
As the wind dances on
Through countless valleys.
This orb becomes an instrument
In the heavens.
It sings a tune that plays just below silence.
Just above wanting.
In between being and becoming.
Just outside of living and dying.
Listen if you can
Beyond every sense you possess
To the whispers of clouds.

## **Dismissed**

The weight of your memory
Sails 'round about me
First here
Then there
Among the trees
Turning ever so softly
In the winds of despair.
For what cause
Or tangled web
Of tinted times gone by
Whisper these branches?
The crisp
Ever familiar
Voice of fall
Comforts me and I call...
Out to you
In the near silent
Din of rustling twigs,
Of leaves.
Provoked:
But in a sense
Dismissed.


## **The Wind O' Pain**

Sitting in the sight
Of faint street lights
At a third story window
Someone remains silently
Half in shadow

Looking upon the world below.
Alone...
Adrift in streams of thought
The wind blows past the pane
As the curtains rise and fall
In a gentle, angelic refrain.
And remaining still he feels
Her hands as the breeze
Sifts through his hair.
A subtle reminder,
Bitter-sweet,
Of a love that isn't there.
With outstretched hands
This mortal band
Reaches out upon the wind
Extending to feel the slope of her ear,
her cheek,
her chin.
The mighty din
Of one thousand distant stars
Shimmer far above...
A teardrop
Skirts the sky
And reminds him
Of her love.


## **Shout**


Must we go out to come in
And go in to come out?
Displacement here
Is placement there.
Perhaps silence is
But the shadow of a shout.

## **Talking Flowers**

The wind blew
Softly upon the heather hills
As I wound my way home
To my love.
Around each bend a new
Spring blossom greeted me
With her smile
And mile after mile
My heart grew fonder
Of that moment when our
Eyes would meet in
Silence (discreet)
Yet full of elegance.

The words might cease
But the memories would linger
Like the slight scent on my fingers
Left behind by the essence of wild flowers.

I picked them one by one
Imagining with each (newly found)
The glorious sound
Of her voice.

I had no choice
But to collect all their
Radiance and beauty
As they swayed in the breeze that day
I heard her calling me.
I felt her smile,

her love,
her laughter.
But when I saw her
I fell silent
As each petal, in their turn, called out:
"I love you,
I love you,
I love you."


## Life's Fluidity Frozen

Life is
As a droplet of water...
Which slips through our fingers
And conforms to the shape
Of the world around it.

Poetry is more
Like an ice crystal...
A frozen droplet of life
Held in hand and closely examined
In every facet.
Poetry is the discovery
Of structure within the fluidity of existence.


## The Heroic Flaw

Solid indeed
Are the cold-faced rocks
That resist the waves of opposition
But such is not the stuff of human endurance,
Of substance,

Of existence.
A granite foundation
May lay waste to the hero
Of human stature
For better a wounded
Man with a golden heart
Than one escaping uninjured
With a heart of stone.


## <u>Over Manhattan</u>


We'll be one small light
Over Manhattan tonight
Hold my hand as we climb, the blue...
(highway in the sky)
We'll rise above the golden rim all right
And skim the wisps of cloud-tops bright
Fold your heart 'round mine, so true...
(only do, never try)
Let's glow with the sun
'til we flow into one
blending into purple hues.


Soaring up on our flight
With the city below now hardly in sight
Mold my visions upon thine, ever new...
(only live, never die)
Let's glow with the sun
'til we flow into one
blending into purple hues.


The blue...
(ever, ever true)
The sky...

(never try, only do)
Glow with the sun
(our love, ever new)
As w flow into one...
(into purple hues)
Blending as we ascend...
(into one).


## A Higher Plane

To take flight
To wander against the wind
And feel the sky press against my face
Is to be at peace with the world.
Amid streams of clouds
And wisps of golden light
My wings caress the heavens
With a softness just short of a touch,
Just below the sound of a heartbeat,
Just above all senses...
On a higher plane.


## Pinwheel-White

A white flower blows across the grass
Along the river-bend
Where my mind took solace
With a friend
Whose memories whispered
Quietly like the pinwheel petals
That dance sweetly toward amend,
Then back again to remembrances
Caught up in the wind.

## **<u>Chamonix</u>**

Oh, bright silver-white colossus
Whose robes brush up against the nearby stream?
In a valley made gold by the morning sun.
How often do I reflect upon you
And ponder your Olympian majesties!
So glorious was the sight to a young boy
Upon waking in Chamonix:
Like a thunderbolt from heaven
Which striking steel grounded my fixation...
As if electrified by the vision:
So grand and powerful,
So cold and foreboding.
Yet decreeing a warm emotion
Upon the villages below,
Where chalets were to be seen here and there
As if carried down with the snow.
And along icy crags and twisty roads
Glaciers of an age gone by
Form mounting aqua waves
Never to recede with the tide.

## **<u>Time Eternal</u>**

There's a clock on an eternal wall
With two hands of the same base;
One determines the first and final hour,
The other snuffs or breathes breath.
As the black arrows go around
In their mechanical way,
Their countless power over the moments to prove,

The hands devour moments by minutes
Until they achieve the terminal velocity of happening.
Alpha and Omega come together in you.

## A Tap on the Shoulder

It's fall again and the spirit calls out
Across the spot where I first saw you;
Around the bend of steps littered leafy-brown
A silent smile of acknowledgment still remains.

It's that time of year when my soul is played
Like a mourning oboe;
A tune that lifts me up on the pathway,
But which dashes me upon the same steps
Which my heart can never ascend.

The feel of fall...
So empty without you
(no falling in love).
The sailing leafs...
So purposeless without you.

Shall I go to that spot where your spirit haunts
And touch the stones over which you once tread?
Will I find one golden thread of your existence?
Oh, Lord ...
What I could have,
Would have,
Should have said!

I remember so well how
The words of your heart
Were like the leafs on the trees,

Falling from your eyes so silently...
Today, an oak-leaf gently came to rest upon my
shoulder
As I passed that spot.
And it, as if an extension of a past time, reminded me
of a day
When I should have been bolder.


## <u>Engagement and Resignation</u>


Eternity touches down at a single point
Coiling itself up into each vital moment.
At those times we can choose
To cast our gaze to the Ultimate Perspective...
Where the dawn and dusk meet to shake hands
Where midday and midnight stand
And greet the forever-now.
Yet so often when the finger of Fate
Reaches down
To touch the ground
We stand there like some helpless sleuth
Searching in vain
For the traces of prints left behind
From the instant of creation
And we draw back in pain and doubt...
Shrinking from the task of perpetual engagement
Seeking instead a quietly detached truth.
But the endless maze of human struggle for discovery
Does not stand as a dark mystery.
Rather, it winds in and around
Life and Being,
Revelation and Meaning
And shines like a priceless medallion
For all who revel in the Ultimate Cause:

The convergence of the moment of creation
With the very instant in which we exist.


## **The Oak**


I shall complain for the elements
Without voices to tell the earth
Of their sorrow.
Of their dismay in growing old.


One day I sighted a grand tree
Along a path much trodden
By youthful figurers
Marching
By a rocky cliff with flowers
Blooming.


Spring was in the air
And that old tree must be feeling the same
Sweet blithe of energy
Coupling through its veins--
Through every succeeding ring
(And for each one the wiser?)


The dark earth buckled
With warm life beneath my boots
(And those of young mountain climbers)
Going up to that place
Where the mountain crags
Meet the skyline.
And there, as if by Heaven's decree,
Stood the lone, majestic oak.


Yet even at this elevation

The roots strike deeply
And its committed strength
Is still able to draw one's view of the world
Into focus despite any swaying.

The wind's soft zephyrs
Slide past the graying
Branches of the oak
And all that listen intently
Can hear the voice of a king
Speaking of the long winter
With the groaning of one hundred years.
A sound like the mast
Of a great and glorious bark.

Of late I have noticed a certain
Leaning in that tree.
Is it I who walk the crooked path?

## Aurora's Path

Give me feathers
So I can perch on a lone, mighty branch
And feel each quill rise
To meet the wind.
I want to measure my soul
Against the horizon
And find it never ending.
Though the sun may set
The distant mountains glow
With the expectation of stars
Which call me on to hover,
Like the wisps of clouds...
To alight upon Aurora's Path

> To soar within the evening shroud
> To sail until the morning's breath
> To lift a wing and conquer death.

**Mary-Ellen:** Did you find anything among these poems that was creepy, or that suggests the writer was a stalker?

[All five girls shrug their shoulders and shake their heads no]

**Laura:** They weren't even all love poems. There's nothing creepy about *any* of them.

**Mary-Ellen:** Anyone disagree? No? Well, *that's it*. We're done. Thanks so much for helping out. You were a BIG help. Your unbiased perspectives have confirmed my view of the matter. I can tell you, now that we're done, I don't think he was a stalker. I've read every single poem and note that he wrote and I've come to the same opinion as you guys.

**Mr. Denker:** Thanks girls.

**Dr. Gallman:** Your parents have all arrived and are waiting for you in the front office. This way out...

**Dani:** Wait. Before we go, could we see a picture of the boy who sent the love poems?

**Mary-Ellen:** Dr. Gallman, may I show them his picture?

**Dr. Gallman:** [Looking at Mr. Denker to see check his opinion] That's fine. Show them a picture if you have one. They could figure out who we've been talking about anyway and then find a yearbook or search Facebook, or go online and search for his obituary and find a picture of Ashley. Go ahead.

**Mary-Ellen:** I have a pic on my iPhone that Paisley modified using Gimp, but it looks just like him. Here you go.

# Ms. Harmony Lehrer

The following is the transcript of my interview with
Ms. Harmony Lehrer, conducted in the guidance office
of Franklin High School, Jedesdorf, PA.

Date: June 20, 2011
Time: 2:40-3:10 PM
Witness: Dr. Lee Gallman (Principal).


**Mary-Ellen:** Ms. Lehrer, would you mind telling me
about your educational background? And about your
teaching experience at Franklin?

**Ms. Lehrer:** Well, I've been teaching high school
English at Franklin High School for 14 years. I worked
at a private academy for one year after attaining my
M.A from DeSales College in Center Valley,
Pennsylvania. Prior to that, I graduated with a double
major from Kutztown University in Pennsylvania. I
majored in English Lit. and Secondary Education.

**Mary-Ellen:** Tell me about the creative writing class
you teach to juniors at Franklin. Was Ashley White in
that class?

**Ms. Lehrer:** That course is quite challenging. Yes,
Ashley White was in that class. He was a promising
writer. He excelled at short stories, screenplays and
poetry. I encouraged him to pursue his talent in
college.

**Mary-Ellen:** What about Marty Fine?  Did you have him in class during his junior year?

**Ms. Lehrer:** Yes, I did.  He was in the same class that I previously mentioned.  Some students, like Marty, thought the class would be an easy A.  They thought writing would be easy.  He—and many others—were disappointed.

**Mary-Ellen:** Tell me about Marty Fine…as a student.

**Ms. Lehrer:** Marty Fine is an "A" student who doesn't have to work hard or study at all to get that grade.  He's a natural leader.  The classes' attitude generally follows his—he sets the tone for *any* class he's in.

Let me clarify:  Marty should get straight A's, but he doesn't.  He received a 76% in the creative writing class, for example.

**Mary-Ellen:** How did he respond to getting a C in your class?

**Ms. Lehrer:** Daddy went on the warpath.  He sent endless emails asking why his son wasn't getting an A. He called me a half-dozen times.  There were two meetings with the principal.

**Mary-Ellen:** Did you give in and give him an A?

**Ms. Lehrer:** No.  His work was sloppy and he rarely put much thought into his writing.  Mr. Fine was adamant that his son deserved an A because Marty's work was "technically superior".

**Mary-Ellen:** You mean, like grammar, punctuation, spelling and style?

**Ms. Lehrer:** Precisely. Marty did master those elements. But I had my suspicions about them. I could never prove it, but his stories and poetry were always about things that he would have no direct knowledge about. It was as if he had paid some college student to write papers for him.

His regular in-class work never approached the quality of what he handed in when it came to long-term assignments. Honestly, I always suspected he cheated on the long-term assignments.

**Mary-Ellen:** Suspected, but never proved?

**Ms. Lehrer:** No, I could never prove it.

**Mary-Ellen:** What about Brenda Waxman? I'm told she was in that class too.

**Ms. Lehrer:** Brenda is intelligent. She's also the most self-centered student I've ever had. It came across in her writing too. She seemed more concerned about her appearance than anything else. *Even her creative writing* reflected an odd obsession with surface stuff. Beyond the writing, she's simply not a nice person. She's cruel to others. I've heard her put other students down. I had to talk about her verbal abuse of others at least twenty times. She's been written up for it…it was often *that* bad. You might want to check with the office on the actual number of times I wrote her up for "cruelty to her fellow classmates", or "creating an intimidating classroom environment for others." It was at least five times.

**Mary-Ellen:** How, exactly, would she intimidate others?

**Ms. Lehrer:** Brenda was always trying to be the center of attention. She put others down—usually girls—in order to build herself up. Her criticisms typically dealt with what other girls looked like…hair, makeup, shoes…oh, yes…and she was quite the gossip. She spent more time spreading rumors than any five girls I know. The rumors usually had something to do with dating.

She sought attention from the boys too. She was flirtatious and wispy. She was continuously playing with her hair, batting her eyelashes, slathering on the lip balm, stretching in such a way as to guarantee the guys around her couldn't help but zero in on her chest, acting pouty, etc.

**Mary-Ellen:** Where her, let's call them, "feminine activities", directed toward getting the attention of any particular guys?

**Ms. Lehrer:** Principally, Marty, her boyfriend. He had this way of egging her on to do more by ignoring her or flirting with other girls. She tried to turn the tables on Marty by flirting with his best friends, like Duwain…and especially Ty.

**Mary-Ellen:** What about Ty Weiser? What was he like in your class?

**Ms. Lehrer:** Ty didn't impress me at all. He was just coasting, academically. He depended too much on his athletic prowess, and his looks. The same thing is true of Ty's "right hand man", Duwain Williams.

Ty and Duwain were followers, in every sense of the word. Although they were popular in their own way because of football and their looks, Marty always had the lion's share of feminine attention. Marty had a certain rich-boy bad-boy swagger that appealed to clueless females.

It seemed like the three guys were constantly in competition to see who could get the freshmen or sophomore girls. They treated it like a game. Get 'em on the hook, take 'em out once or twice, then drop 'em like a hot potato, and laugh at them when they came to school every day thereafter for a week in tears. *Oh, the drama.*

Duwain and Trudy were dating, despite Duwain's constantly cheating on her.

It's amazing what you overhear as a teacher, isn't it?

**Mary-Ellen:** It sure is. What about Trudy Schroeder? You mentioned Trudy. What was she like in class?

**Ms. Lehrer:** Trudy's a sycophant, plain and simple. She does whatever Brenda and Marty direct her to do. She's a non-student. I'm sorry to sound so negative, but was constantly waffling, going back and forth between having a modicum of self awareness...and days and days of obliviousness.

It seemed like every time she took one step forward, the next day it was 20 steps back. I know there's a conscious in there somewhere, but it was always overshadowed by the opposite that it's hard for me to even put in word what I've observed...regarding her lack of a conscious, that is.

**Mary-Ellen:** Interesting. Would you mind trying to explain what you mean about Trudy?

**Ms. Lehrer:** How can I put this?....You know, in a literature class there are times when kids get a lot out of discussions about social issues. Great literature struggles with the conflict of the human spirit, with societal problems, with clashes of personality, with events that are character building.

Well, every once in a while, Trudy would seem to have a breakthrough. She would, or so it seemed, have a moment of clarity. She'd have a moment where she could actually sympathize or empathize with the struggles of others...and then...

**Mary-Ellen:** Then...?

**Ms. Lehrer:** Two seconds later she'd say something so far off the wall, off topic, or simply vacuous, that I would have to shake my head and wonder internally, *is this the same girl who just spoke moments ago as if she could actually care about someone other than herself?*

Maybe you'd have to be there to witness it for yourself. It's quite baffling behavior. Trudy had these moments...then two minutes later she'd make fun of her prior position, opinions, etc.

**Mary-Ellen:** OK. I get the picture. I know two girls just like that. It's as if they realize that having a heart isn't cool and then go out of their way to assure themselves and everyone else what stereotype they fit into. They get uncomfortable with the idea of personal growth.

**Ms. Lehrer:** Very insightful, Mary-Ellen. That's exactly the way Trudy is.

**Mary-Ellen:** Enough about Trudy; tell me about Ashley White?

**Ms. Lehrer:** Ashley was one of the best students I've ever had. He was an excellent writer. He was a bit on the quiet side, but he had started to develop more confidence and come out of his shell in the spring of his junior year. He was a thoughtful, considerate and sensitive person. His writing reflected advanced sensibilities.

**Mary-Ellen:** The posting of the poem on your wall must have horrified him.

**Ms. Lehrer:** He was devastated. In all my years of teaching, I've never seen a student more embarrassed by a single event…and I've seen a lot of unusual, embarrassing things along the way.

**Mary-Ellen:** You've obviously heard about the prank. You've heard about the unloosening of one of your chairs so Ashley would get up on the chair, it would collapse, etc. So, who perpetrated this prank on Ashley?

**Ms. Lehrer:** I honestly didn't see who rigged the chair and posted the poem. I was out in the hallway with Trudy and Brenda.

**Mary-Ellen:** What does your gut tell you? Who would have done something like that?

**Ms. Lehrer:** My instincts inform me that it would be Brenda and Marty. Brenda was with me in the hallway. That means she didn't—physically—loosen the bolts and screws on the chair and post the poem, but it seems like the sort of thing she'd come up with. Marty did the actual dirty work, probably with Duwain or Ty's assistance.

**Mary-Ellen:** Was your class unattended and unlocked during lunch that day?

**Ms. Lehrer:** On Monday, May 13?

**Mary-Ellen:** Yes.

**Ms. Lehrer:** I did leave my classroom during the lunch period. It was unlocked. I never used to lock my classroom and, up to that day, I had never had anyone go into my unattended classroom and take things.

**Mary-Ellen:** Tell me exactly what happened as you stood in the hallway after lunch—before class began that day.

**Ms. Lehrer:** After lunch I stood in the hallway as the students filed in. Two students kept me out in the hallway with all sorts of questions.

**Mary-Ellen:** Just to clarify, who…

**Ms. Lehrer:** Brenda Waxman & Trudy Schroeder.

**Mary-Ellen:** Thanks. Give me your best, most detailed account of what happened after this conversation—when you entered the classroom.

**Ms. Lehrer:** After taking attendance on my laptop, I walked to the head of the classroom and looked to see if anyone had posted writing. There's a poster located to the left of my desk about half-way up the wall. Students volunteer to post things they've written there for extra credit. Someone had moved the poster to a significantly higher position on the wall—probably a good two feet higher than it typically is. I saw Ashley's name on a poem posted on it and asked him if he'd be willing to share it with the whole class. I thought nothing of it. He had posted poems there several times before. But this time his reaction was very different.

**Mary-Ellen:** How so?

**Ms. Lehrer:** He got a terrified look on his face and went into panic mode, running to the head of the class and jumping up on a chair under the poster in an effort to tear it down. The chair collapsed and Ashley fell. As he fell, Ashley struck his head on a nearby heater/AC unit.

**Mary-Ellen:** He struck his head?

**Ms. Lehrer:** He sure did. Many in the class thought it was a comical scene and laughed at his panic and fall. Ashley fell to the floor and didn't move. I ran to him. He was on his back and a welt was already forming on his forehead, above his left eye. He didn't seem to be breathing. His chest did not rise and fall. I gently checked his eyes and noticed one of his pupils was larger than the other. I grabbed his wrist and found a weak pulse. Just then, Ashley took a deep breath and sat up. It was like he was jolted from a nightmare. He was dazed and confused, and scrambled to his feet. He stumbled across the classroom and stuffed the crumpled poem into his pocket. He was not responsive to my questions or anyone else's comments, so I phoned the nurse. I demanded that she come down to my room immediately. It told her to bring an ice pack.

**Mary-Ellen:** When Ashley jumped up, what did he say and do?

**Ms. Lehrer:** The class was awkwardly silent as Ashley yelled at the class during the minute it took for the nurse to show up. When the nurse arrived Ashley didn't want to go with her. He ran out the door with the nurse running after him. I ran to the end of the senior hallway until I saw him corralled by the principal, Dr. Gallman, and the guidance counselor, Mr. Denker, and the nurse. Then I returned to my classroom.

**Mary-Ellen:** What happened to Ashley after that?

**Ms. Lehrer:** I don't know what happened to him after that, although I talked to the principal after school and he told me that Ashley had left school in his car around 2:30 and that nobody knew where he was going.

**Mary-Ellen:** What about the kids in your room? What did they say or do when you got back?

**Ms. Lehrer:** After Ashley left the class I remember a few students still thought it was funny. Brenda, Marty and Duwain chuckled into their hands. Trudy cried and Ty looked terrified.

I confronted them about the poem. Nobody would admit to posting Ashley's secret admirer poem, even though I sternly lectured the class about their cruelty for the remainder of the period.

After class, a boy who asked not to be revealed told me he had seen Marty "rig Ashley's accidental fall."

**Mary-Ellen:** There must have been others who saw what Marty, Ty and Duwain did with the chair and the poem.

**Ms. Lehrer:** No doubt about it. That's how intimidating Marty and his buddies can be. Nobody wanted to be on Marty's bad side. Nobody wanted to be a target.

**Mary-Ellen:** Why do you suppose Marty never got caught...for anything. I mean...all these years he's been pretty much terrorizing others and he has no disciplinary record whatsoever. How can this be?

**Ms. Lehrer:** He's a real charmer. He seemed to be able to talk his way out of anything. He's a professional liar too...Pathological in my estimation. I guess the students he picked on learned not to take these matters to the office after a while because Marty somehow could always weasel his way out of whatever trouble he was in...and then he'd be back with a vengeance...twice as sneaky, twice as crafty, and three times more careful. He was a master manipulator and planner. He'd get back at whoever tried to get him in trouble, and he'd do it in such a subtle way that it couldn't be traced to him.

**Mary-Ellen:** Or he'd get his stooges to take the fall.

**Ms. Lehrer:** So true.  Look at how many detentions and suspensions are on Duwain, Ty or Trudy's records...stooges indeed.

**Mary-Ellen:** You'd think that Marty's friends would get tired of taking the blame for the things *he* actually did?

**Ms. Lehrer:** That's the trick, though.  You see, Marty comes up with an idea to do something, draws his friends in, manipulates the conversation to make it seem like *they* came up with the idea/plan...and then sits back and watches it all unfold.

**Mary-Ellen:** Ok, but you mentioned a few minutes ago something about the boy who came to you after class and told you to keep in on the down-low, but that he saw Marty actually setting up the chair and poem on the poster in your classroom. That sounds like Marty wasn't just sitting back and watching his stooges do all the physical work.

**Ms. Lehrer:** Well, the boy who came to me after class never actually said something like, "I saw Marty unscrewing the chair so it would collapse."  What he said was closer to, "I saw Marty get out his pocket knife.  It had a screw driver on it. Then they unscrewed the chair and placed it under the poster, where they had already hung up Ashley's poem in a place where Ashley would have to get up on the chair to remove it."  Now, mind you, I'm paraphrasing.

**Mary-Ellen:** Sure, I understand.  There's no way you could remember, word-for-word, what this boy told you.

**Ms. Lehrer:** I must get going, Mary-Ellen. I hope I've been helpful. Go get 'em! I understand no criminal charges are pending in this case, but you can use the power of the pen in an instructive way. Maybe what you will write about in this matter will save someone's life. You never know.

**Mary-Ellen:** I want to show you a picture of your classroom taken of your classroom by the police. They re-hung the poem and put the chair back where it was prior to its collapse. Would you simply verify whether this is indeed what your classroom looked like on May 13, 2011?

**Ms. Lehrer:** Certainly.

**Mary-Ellen:** Here you go.

**Ms. Lehrer:** Yes. That's the way it was. Ashley was seated in the desk at the bottom left corner. You can see the poster hanging on the wall behind my desk, and, to the left, the filing cabinet Ashley smacked his head on when the chair collapsed and he fell.

**Mary-Ellen:** You've been a big help, Ms. Lehrer...and I hope you're right about the power of the pen. Ashley was a nice guy. He didn't deserve what happened to him in your class...or later on that day.

## Paisley Wahr

The following is the transcript of my interview with
Paisley Wahr, conducted in the guidance office of
Franklin High School, Jedesdorf, PA.

Date:  June 20, 2011
Time:  2:40-3:37 PM
Witness:  Mr. Denker (Guidance Counselor).


**Mary-Ellen:**  I saw one of your acrylics hanging in the
main hall yesterday.  I wanted to tell you how
impressed I was.  You're really talented.

**Paisley:**  Thanks.  I love to paint.

**Mary-Ellen:**  I hear you are a good writer too.

**Paisley:**  I like to write.  I'm not a great writer yet, but
I'm working on it.  Now, Ashley was a great writer.

**Mary-Ellen:**  You guys were really close, weren't you?

**Paisley:**  Ashley was my best friend since we met in 5th
grade.  He was a quiet, shy boy when I first met him.
He had moved from South Carolina that summer
between fourth and fifth grades.  He felt like a misfit,
particularly because people made fun of him for
"having a girl's name."

**Mary-Ellen:** Why do you think his mom and dad gave him a girl's name?  Surely they knew that would be brutal.

**Paisley:** Actually, in the South it is a boy's name. Ashley was named after a family member who was a founder of the Carolina colony, back in the 17th century.  Ashley…Anthony Ashley Cooper that is. Ashley told me that Lord Ashley was an important advisor to King Charles II.

Ashley and his Dad loved to talk about their family's history.  They were very proud of it and did a lot of research on their family tree.

Ashley and I became friends in September of our 5th grade year.  He was a sweet, intelligent guy and a loyal friend.  I miss him.  Life hasn't been the same.

**Mary-Ellen:** Did you know that Ashley suffered from depression in high school?

**Paisley:** I had no idea he was depressed.  He never mentioned anything about being on medication for depression.  He did talk about "being ugly" and sometimes referred to himself as having a "pizza face". He was very self-conscious about his acne in 8th grade. It went away by the end of 9th grade though.  There was nothing wrong with his face after that.

**Mary-Ellen:** So, even after his acne had gone away, he was still very self-conscious and lacked confidence.  He must have had enough confidence to pursue M&M… right?

**Paisley:** Not really.  He was afraid of being rejected. If a person has real self-confidence, they'll just walk right up to the person they have a crush on and tell them. Or maybe send a text message, or hit them up on Facebook. Ashley was so worried about being rejected by M&M that he apparently felt the only way to approach her was anonymously.

**Mary-Ellen:** Did you play any role in encouraging Ashley to approach M&M?

**Paisley:** Yes. When he told me about his determination to somehow let her know he liked her, I recommended that he put his best foot forward by writing her something. I said writing her a poem was probably the best idea.

**Mary-Ellen:** He write her a poem soon after that conversation, didn't he? But he didn't put his name to it. Right?

**Paisley:** I told him not to fear signing his name to the poem, but Ashley was not only concerned with being rejected by M&M. He was also afraid of what her friends would *do* to him.

Over a period of months, Ashley put dozens of poems and cards and letters signed "Yours, Anonymous" or "Your Secret Admirer" in Mary Margaret's locker.

**Mary-Ellen:** Tell me about the first morning when he dropped off the first note. It was a Valentine's note.

**Paisley:** Since we were at school earlier than everyone else for band practice, it gave Ashley a chance to stick the note in the slats in Mary Margaret's locker without being seen by others.

**Mary-Ellen:** Is this the note?

M&M,
Your beauty leaves me speechless.
Have a great Valentine's Day!
Yours,
Anonymous

**Paisley:** That's the note. It was attached to a red rose that he paid to have delivered to her in homeroom on Valentine's Day.

**Mary-Ellen:** Did he continue to put notes and poems in her locker after Valentine's Day?

**Paisley:** Yes, she publicly bragged about receiving them. This response encouraged him to write and deliver more and more.

**Mary-Ellen:** How many more?

**Paisley:** Perhaps a dozen.

**Mary-Ellen:** Were they all signed, "Yours, Anonymous"?

**Paisley:** Yes, he never revealed his true identity as far as I know. Although he did speculate that she would certainly figure it out eventually.

**Mary-Ellen:** Did he drop hints in some of the letters?

**Paisley:**  I suspect he thought the poems were a huge hint.  After all, he was the only guy known for writing poetry in our class.

**Mary-Ellen:**  Understood. Now, let's fast forward a bit.  Tell me what you remember about the lunch period on Monday, May 13.

**Paisley:**  Well, it was pretty much like any other day until we came back from returning our trays.  Someone had left a chocolate milk carton for Ashley.

**Mary-Ellen:**  Was it just the two of you?  Were there others at your lunch table?

**Paisley:**  No.  We were the only two at our table that day.  Actually, it's usually just the two of us.

**Mary-Ellen:**  Tell me all about it.

**Paisley:**  I was with him at lunch when someone left a carton of chocolate milk with a sticky note on it.  Ashley shared what it said.  It was signed by Mary Margaret, saying she knew all along who was behind the mysterious secret admirer notes and that she was "very touched by the beautiful poems".  The note from Mary Margaret was a thank you note and she revealed that she had been watching him too for a few weeks and knew how much he loved chocolate milk.

**Mary-Ellen:**  You told me once before that you used your iPhone to take a pic of the chocolate milk Ashley received.  Do you still have it?

**Paisley:**  Yep, here you go.

**Mary-Ellen:**  Did Ashley drink the milk?

**Paisley:**  Of course.

**Mary-Ellen:**  Did he make any comments about the chocolate milk tasting strange?

**Paisley:**  He chugged it right down.  After, he said something about it being bitter and he wondered if it had gone bad.   He also said it was warm.  But Ashley was the happiest I had ever seen him and he drank the chocolate milk like it was the best drink ever. It had a yellow Post-it note on the bottom, signed by M&M. He was acting as if he thought she might be watching. Even if it did taste horrible, I don't think he would have ever let on about it. He told me that he might even have the guts to actually walk right up to her and say hello and thanks.  When he left I was sure he was going directly to talk with her, but I don't know where he went or whether M&M was in his 6th period class.

**Mary-Ellen:** She wasn't. Were you?

**Paisley:** No.

**Mary-Ellen:** So, lunch was the last time you saw Ashley?

**Paisley:** The last time.

**Mary-Ellen:** He was seen racing out of the school parking lot. The police accident report indicates Ashley was driving recklessly. Have you ever been a passenger in Ashley's car? Was he ever reckless?

**Paisley:** I knew Ashley better than anyone did and I've driven with him hundreds of times. He was always careful and *never* drove recklessly.

**Mary-Ellen:** If he had taken any drugs that day, perhaps it affected his thinking? The autopsy found ecstasy in his system.

**Paisley:** He never took drugs and never went to parties where he knew there would be drugs—like Marty Fine's parties. He thought the parties were stupid and for shallow, self-centered and stuck up people.

**Mary-Ellen:** You really don't know who left the chocolate milk on the table, do you? Do you think it came from M&M, like the note said?

**Paisley:** I thought it did, at the time anyway. Now, I think someone like Brenda or Marty put it on the table. I think they spiked the chocolate milk with ecstasy to embarrass Ashley. Maybe they wanted to get him in trouble. Maybe they thought he would go to class and get sent to the nurse for acting high and get busted. Maybe they wanted him to be out of his mind so by the time he was in class they could embarrass him by posting one of his love notes to M&M. That's what everyone in the class says happened. I figure Marty, Brenda and their jerk friends were trying to "put Ashley in his place" for writing all those notes and poems to M&M.

**Mary-Ellen:** What makes you think Brenda Waxman had anything to do with what happened in class?

**Paisley:** Of all the classmates that Ashley disliked, he disliked Brenda Waxman the most. He stood up to her several times in our sophomore and junior years. I remember one time he walked up to her and called her "The biggest two-faced fake in the school". He never could understand why M&M would hang out with such a "stuck up witch". M&M was so nice to everyone. Brenda was always making fun of Ashley and anyone else who was like him.

**Mary-Ellen:** Did she make fun of you?

**Paisley:** Yes. In fact, the time that I mentioned that he confronted her, was in response to her vicious attitude toward me.

**Mary-Ellen:** What did she say or do to you that provoked Ashley to call Brenda a "two-faced fake"?

**Paisley:** She pretended to be my friend for like a week. We talked a lot and I told her that my Dad was in prison for writing bad checks. Brenda told *everyone* that my dad was really in prison for *molesting* me.

**Mary-Ellen:** That's horrible.

**Paisley:** Yeah. Horrible. Ashley stood up for me. I love…loved him for that.

**Mary-Ellen:** Tell me the truth. Did you have romantic feelings for Ashley?

**Paisley:** Yes…but now he's gone forever.

**Mary-Ellen:** I'm so Sorry, Paisley.

**Paisley:** No more questions. Okay?

**Mary-Ellen:** Of course. Again, I'm Sorry. He was a great guy. No doubt.

**Paisley:** He wouldn't have committed suicide, or drugged himself up so he could kill himself. Understand?

**Mary-Ellen:** I believe you, hon.

**Paisley:** Thanks. I hope you make them pay for what they did to Ashley. If they don't pay, they'll do it again.

**Mary-Ellen:** That's exactly why I'm doing these interviews and writing this book. Maybe the DA will re-open the case after they get pressure from the community.  I'm going to take this to TV talk shows, if that's what it takes to get the word out and provoke the authorities to reconsider the case.

**Paisley:** Thanks.  Best of luck.  If you ever need me to speak out, I'm there for you.

**Mary-Ellen:** Thanks. I appreciate that.  You know, I honestly believe that if Ashley had known you loved him that this M&M thing would never have developed.

**Paisley:**  I live with that disturbing thought every day, Mary-Ellen.  It's been eating me alive ever since he died.  If only I had told him that I loved him.

**Mary-Ellen:**  Yeah.  But how were you supposed to know that Marty and his friends would do something so god-awful horrid?  There's no way you could have foreseen that Ashley would end up dead.

**Paisley:**  I suppose you're right.  Thanks for saying that.

**Mary-Ellen:**  I'll see you later.

**Paisley:**  Wait.  Do you have a lap top in your bag?

**Mary-Ellen:**  Yes. Why?

**Paisley:**  I just now thought of something that you should see.  Did you know that Ashley had a Facebook page?

**Mary-Ellen:**  No...and....

**Paisley:** It's still up. Nobody ever took it down.

**Mary-Ellen:** You're serious.

**Paisley:** Yeah. Since I was one of his few Facebook friends, I could actually show you what's on his page. His Facebook settings didn't allow non-friends to find him or to see his page.

**Mary-Ellen:** Heck yes, I want to see it. I think it will be blocked on the school server, though.

**Mr. Denker:** You girls will have to go home for that. Facebook is blocked and I don't have the authority to un-block it for you.

**Paisley:** Follow me to my house. It's not far from here.

**Mary-Ellen:** Great! Let's go.

# Paisley Wahr, Part 2

The following is the transcript of my continued interview with Paisley Wahr, conducted at her home in Jedesdorf, PA.

Date:  June 20, 2011
Time:  4:00-5:15 PM
Witness:
   No adult witness present. Dated screen shots have been taken.  These are available as proof of the accuracy of the material I harvested from Ashley White's Facebook page.  These screen shots will not be included in this report.  However, they are available upon request.
   As of the publishing of this book, Ashley White's Facebook page has been removed at the request of his parents.

**Mary-Ellen**:  Ashley only has ten Facebook friends, including you.

**Paisley:**  He didn't have many friends at school either, as you obviously know by now.

**Mary-Ellen:**  Before we check out any conversations between Ashley and his friends, could we look at anything that he posted that is more substantial, like notes or events?

**Paisley:**  Sure.

**Mary-Ellen:**  Wait a minute. Are you kidding me?  Go back.  Isn't that M&M?

**Paisley:**  Yes.

**Mary-Ellen:**  They were Facebook friends?

**Paisley:**  Yes.

**Mary-Ellen:**  For how long?

**Paisley:**  Let's see...Um...from May 5 of their senior year.

**Mary-Ellen:**  That's just a couple of weeks before his accident.  You mean they were Facebook friends and somehow she couldn't figure out that Ashley was her secret admirer?  That's crazy.

**Paisley:**  For sure.  Crazy.  Look at these.  When you see these, you'll see just how crazy it was that she didn't figure it out.  See all of these notes?

**Mary-Ellen:**  Those are his poems.  All of them.  He was posting them as notes to his Facebook friends a week—no, three days—before the crash!  This doesn't make sense!

**Paisley:**  Take a look at this.  It's an explanation of a book of poetry he was putting together.  He put it right out there in a Facebook note to all 10 friends.  M&M would have received this two days before the accident. The Facebook note's title is "Silent Words."  Could he have been more obvious?

++BEGIN COPY/PASTED TEXT++

## SILENT WORDS by Ashley White

"Dear friends, SILENT WORDS represents my quest to understand the world—a journey that never seems to end.

Admittedly, there are no answers among my words, only measurements, attempts to place myself alongside you and your infinite complexities and draw finite insights and conclusions.

I have learned much about the world recently by remaining silent and watching and refraining from comment. I've allowed people, places and events to unfold on their own time. By silencing my natural tendency to evaluate everything and everyone, I've learned to feel the truth cropping up among the events. It has made me more optimistic. It has created a certain emotional buoyancy when I simply stand back and allow the ones I love and admire to shine. I write through them. Maybe, my friend, I've written because of the wonder that is YOU.

When the notion of sustained silence becomes insufferable the words just come along—from start to finish. Any other way feels forced. You are an inspiration to me without even knowing it.

Initially, I was silent because I was afraid to reveal the truth—afraid of rejection. Eventually the fear melted away. It was replaced by observation. I'm hoping that you will read my poems and be kind enough to return the favor. Will you make observations and tell me what you think of them?

During this journey, there have been many happy accidents and observations along the way.

These poems are the result.  I hope that you will find meaning and truth in my silence.

++END COPY/PASTED TEXT++

**Mary-Ellen:**  I can't believe this.  You...everyone commented on these poems Ashley posted.  Everyone, that is, except M&M.  [scrolling down] 10 friends received this note and nine responded, multiple times.

**Paisley:**  Look at my comment. See, Thumbs Up, and...

++BEGIN COPY/PASTED TEXT++

Well, done my friend :)  My faves r def the less lovey-dovey ones ;) Do you think she'll figure it out?  Does she read ur posts?

++END COPY/PASTED TEXT++

**Mary-Ellen:**  Who is this guy?

**Paisley:**  That's Max.  He was in the marching band with Ashley.  They both played Tuba.  Check out the pics.

**Mary-Ellen:**  I've never actually seen pics of Ashley in his band uniform. He looks so happy.  The guy next to him must be Max.

**Paisley:**  Yep.  The two of them would do the most incredible act at the end of games.  They called it "Florida A&M—the Caucasian Edition." It's so funny.

If we go to Max's page I think he's got a couple clips posted. Wanna see?

**Mary-Ellen:** Yes. Why "Florida A&M?" I'm not familiar with the reference. It must be a bando thing.

**Paisley:** Bando thing...*to the core.* You've never seen a clip of the Florida A&M band playing a football halftime show?

**Mary-Ellen:** Can't say that I have.

**Paisley:** You've been deprived. Ok, so first things first. You've gotta see a Youtube clip of the FAMU band. Then it will make sense.

https://www.youtube.com/watch?v=ydVswV8R0TI

**Mary-Ellen:** What an amazing band. I have to admit that I'd never even heard of Florida A&M University.

**Paisley:** Ashley could be very silly, especially around that big goof, Max. Watch this clip of Ashley and Max.

https://www.youtube.com/watch?x=v2xsVr8888
(Sorry, this video was removed in December of 2011, at Ashley's parent's request)

**Mary-Ellen:** Incredible. That explains a lot! Ashley really did have a funny side to him, didn't he?
**Paisley:** He sure did. Take a look at M&M's Facebook page. Strange, huh? She only has a handful of friends on here.

**Mary-Ellen:** That is strange. Miss popular only has 25 Facebook friends? What's up with that? Looks like she rarely goes on Facebook. Let's see...her last post was in May of 2011. Hum...no Marty, no Brenda, no Duwain, no Ty, no...none of her clique. It might just be family. She told me her dad was strict. Sure looks like she wasn't exaggerating that one.

**Paisley:** Sorry to interrupt, but...you have to see these pics.

**Mary-Ellen:** Oh, yeah, those are all from school. Did Ashley take these with his iPhone?

**Paisley:** Yes, there are videos too. Look at this one. You're gonna flip.

**Mary-Ellen:** What?! That's Marty Fine and Duwain. What are they doing with those blue shorts?

**Paisley:** Ashley discretely shot this in the locker room after gym class one day. You remember the kid they called, Dumbo?

**Mary-Ellen:** No. Dumbo?

**Paisley:** The shorts they got out of the locker belong to Tommy Tombeaux, aka, Tommy "Dumbo". See what they are sprinkling?

**Mary-Ellen:** Looks like a baby powder bottle.

**Paisley:** Think again. Think prank.

**Mary-Ellen:** Itching powder?

**Paisley:** Bingo. Give that girl a prize. Ashley overheard Marty bragging about putting okra in a small foot powder bottle and saying he was going to put the okra powder "in Dumbo's short and underwear."

**Mary-Ellen:** What? Okra powder? Isn't okra a cooking spice, like for gumbo?

**Paisley:** Yes. Apparently, Marty spent quality time researching alternative uses for okra. Ashley has seen Marty with it in class, sprinkling it on other kids' seats. What a jerk, huh?

**Mary-Ellen:** What a jerk is right. Unbelievable. You know, several people have told me some "Marty stories" in the course of these interviews, but this is the first time I've run across actual evidence.

**Paisley:** Look here. See Ashley's friends? That's Tommy. He uses "Dumbo the Elephant" as his Facebook pic. See?

**Mary-Ellen:** Why? Why would anybody do that?

**Paisley:** He's the kind of guy who just goes with it. You know, thinking it's better to play along, rather than invite more persecution. Friggin' Marty has played practical jokes on dozens of kids and teachers, but he has probably done more crap to Tommy than all the rest—combined.

**Mary-Ellen:** Why Tommy? Do you think Tommy would do an interview?

**Paisley:** Because Tommy is "fat and jolly." No matter what Marty and his piss-ant buddies ever did to Tommy, Tommy chuckles and chuckles and chuckles and chuckles. Have you ever heard a guy that sounds like a demented clown, stuck inside a cuckoo clock, when he laughs?

**Mary-Ellen:** Honestly, that does sound annoying.

**Paisley:** It is, and Tommy knows it. He does it on purpose to annoy people or make people laugh. He really is a nice guy. I think he's created this whole doofus persona to mask the hurt. He could tell you some nasty stories about Marty and his friends.

**Mary-Ellen:** Would you call Tommy and ask him if he'd be willing to participate in an interview with me?

**Paisley:** I'll call him tonight and get back to you. I know he'll do it. He hates Marty and he never misses an opportunity to tell a story.

**Mary-Ellen:** Thanks. Tonight, would you please email me copies of the screen shots of Ashley's Facebook page? I have to go. I promised my father that I'd be home in time for dinner tonight. It's his birthday.

**Paisley:** Consider it done. See you later.

**Mary-Ellen:** Later. I'm going to have to pay a visit to Mary Margaret Dolce tomorrow afternoon and ask her how the heck she never figured out who was sending her the anonymous poems, since she was friends with Ashley on Facebook.

**Paisley:** Yeah, she's got some 'splainin' to do. Please let me know what she says, I've been curious about that for a long time.

**Mary-Ellen:** Later.

# Mary Margaret Dolce, pt. 2

The following is the transcript of my second interview with Mary Margaret Dolce, conducted at her home in Jedesdorf, PA.

Date:  June 21, 2011
Time:  5:00-6:00 PM
Witness: Mr. Frank Dolce (M&M's father)

**Mary-Ellen:**  Thanks for agreeing to another brief interview, M&M.  I have a few items that have been bugging me since the last time we talked.  One thing in particular doesn't add up.

**Mary Margaret:**  What doesn't add up?

**Mary-Ellen:**  I've discovered that you and Ashley were Facebook friends.

**Mary Margaret:**  Yes.  So?

**Mr. Dolce:**  Holds on...M&M, didn't I say you weren't allowed to use Facepage for people outside of our family?  Were you leading the boy on?

**Mary Margaret:** No, daddy, I wasn't leading Ashley on.  I'm sorry.  He was the only one, and we almost never communicated.  Maybe a few times, that's it, I promise.

**Mary-Ellen:** Mr. Dolce, I have seen Ashley's page and I can verify she's telling the truth.  I couldn't access any private messages between them, but I can tell you that they only wrote on each other's walls a few times.

**Mr. Dolce:** That's good to know, Mary-Ellen. I don't have a Facepage, so I'm not up on "writing on walls" and any other dang thing about it.

**Mary-Ellen:** M&M, since your Facebook page was set to private, and nobody who wasn't your friend could tell you even had an account, how did you end up with Ashley as a friend?

**Mary Margaret:** I searched for him on Facebook, found him and sent him a friend request. He accepted.

**Mary-Ellen:** Wait. Are you telling me that—out of the blue—of all the boys at Franklin you could have friended on Facebook, you reached out to Ashley White? Why?

**Mary Margaret:** Somehow he knew I was having big time trouble with a term paper for Mr. Hogan history class. One day he came up to me in the hallway. He said he overheard me complaining to Mr. Hogan about the term paper. Ashley said he could help. We met in the school library, that same day after school. We brainstormed to come up with a thesis statement, and an outline. He even helped me round up a few books to get started. Nobody has ever reached out to me like that, just to be helpful. And he barely knew me.

**Mr. Dolce:** Well, I'm afraid his intentions weren't quite as pure as you make it sound, my dear, naïve girl. He was the guy writing you all the mushy stuff after all.

**Mary Margaret:** Daddy, I had no idea Ashley thought of me...

**Mary-Ellen:** Hold up. How could you NOT know? Ashley posted all of his poems to his Facebook page, where you could have read them at any time. He posted a rather long note to all of his friends there too. He even re-posted it as an event and invited *you* to read it. I have proof—*look at this screenshot.* You *received* this invitation and *responded.* See that's your face among the others listed who 'attended' this online Facebook event. Now tell me, tell us, how did you NOT know? The poems he sent you were among the ones that he posted. In fact, all the poems he put in your locker at school were among those he posted in this note. By this response, you led him to believe that you had read it.

**Mary Margaret:** I fibbed. I never read it. Sorry. I know that sounds terrible, but it's the God-honest truth.

**Mr. Dolce:** What? How in blazes can you attend an event on line? And furthermore, how can a note be an event? My head is about to explode from the sheer stupidity of it all! This is why I didn't want you on that blasted thing. It's an open invitation for trouble.

**Mary-Ellen:** Well, M&M, I can't prove that you actually read the note. If you really did, then you'll have to live with that lie for the rest of your life.

**Mary Margaret:** Please don't include this in your...

**Mary-Ellen:** You can be sure it will be. Try to stop me.

**Mary Margaret:** I'm so sorry, Mary-Ellen. Please forgive me. I'm telling you the truth. It makes me sound so shallow, I know. I didn't read even one word of it.

**Mary-Ellen:** Ok...you have admitted to being s curious about whom these love poems were coming from. Does that only apply when the author is afraid to put his name on it?

**Mary Margaret:** Don't be cruel. That's not fair. Just because Ashley invites me on Facebook to read poetry he's written doesn't mean the other poems had to be coming from him.

**Mary-Ellen:** You're missing the point. Tell me this: who else, **ever**, has sent you poetry?

**Mary Margaret:** Nobody.

**Mary-Ellen:** Right. Nobody. It seems to me that your curiosity should have been aroused by this Facebook event invitation. But....no?

**Mary Margaret:** No, see [pointing to the screen shot on Mary-Ellen's iPhone]; look when it was sent. It was sent on *that* Sunday night in May. You know, the next day is when Ashley left school after the prank and crashed his car. Even if I had wanted to read it, I wouldn't have had time to read it before Ashley was in the accident.

**Mary-Ellen:** Why didn't you tell me about this when we spoke the first time? It seems suspicious. Maybe you *did* message him in private, and maybe you *did* read the poems and connect the dots...and maybe you wrote something nasty to him.

**Mary Margaret:** I didn't tell you the first time because I knew it would make me look bad; make me look shallow and heartless.

**Mary-Ellen:** So, are you willing to go on Facebook right in front of me, and your father, and show us your message history?

**Mary Margaret:** Yes. Daddy, where's Mom's Mac?

**Mr. Dolce:** I'll be right back.

[Approximately 5 minutes later]

**Mary Margaret:** See. Here are all of my private messages. I've got one from Aunt Irene from last February. That's it. Satisfied?

**Mary-Ellen:** Not really.

**Mary Margaret:** Why? You've seen the truth with your own two eyes.

**Mary-Ellen:** M&M. C'mon now. Anyone can delete these messages. I'd probably have to get a court order to force Facebook to recover deleted messages. That's never going to happen.

**Mr. Dolce:** That's *not* going to happen, little miss District Attorney. I think we've had about all we need to hear from you, today...or ever. It's time for you to leave this house.

M&M, I think you should delete the entire Facebook account. This thing is nothing but trouble.

**Mary-Ellen:** Fine. Good-bye.

**Mr. Dolce:** Before you go, Mary-Ellen, I want to make something clear to you: I don't want you publishing this interview. We do not consent.

**Mary-Ellen:** So sue me! Then, during my defense, I can bring out in civil court what the DA refuses to bring to criminal court.

# Tommy Tombeaux

The following is the transcript of my interview with Tommy Tombeaux, conducted at his home in Jedesdorf, PA.

Date:  June 22, 2011
Time:  3:30-4:15 PM
Witness:  Mrs. Betty Tombeaux (Tommy's Mom)

**Mary-Ellen:**  Thanks for letting me come over to your beautiful house to do the interview.  Mrs. Tombeaux, you sure do have a green thumb. This place looks like it belongs in a magazine.  Are you sure someone actually lives here?

**Mrs. Tombeaux:**  How sweet of you to say.  Thanks. Tommy actually helps me with the gardening.  He's going to make one heck of a landscaper.

**Tommy:**  Yeah, "Dumbo & Son's landscaping".  Very catchy.  Right?

**Mary-Ellen:**  Very funny, Tommy.  Paisley warned me about your self-effacing sense of humor.
  All I really want to talk to you about today is how Marty Fine treated you in middle school and high school.  I want all the details.  And if you know of other cases, things that have happened to other kids, don't hesitate to tell me about those incidents too.

**Tommy:** The word that comes to mind when I think about Marty and his minions is...Mom, 'ear muffs'. Mom, seriously ... 'ear muffs' *now*!

[Mrs. Tombeaux smiled and placed both hands over her ears until Tommy filled in the missing word and gave her the all clear sign]

**Mary-Ellen:** So...it's safe to say you're not fond of Mr. Fine.

**Tommy:** That's probably the biggest understatement of my school experience.

**Mary-Ellen:** OK, then, *let it rip*. Let's do this in chronological order. Start in middle school and give me a flavor for what Marty's & his "minions" did to you, and others.

**Tommy:** "Marty & His Minions"...sounds like the name of a band. He did have a 'band' too, you know. I'll get to that, later. He didn't have a 'band' until our senior year.

Middle school, eh...I've got one for you.

The dumb stuff was constant. Ty and Duwain would help tackle me and then Marty would sit on my face and **fart**...stuff like that. But those kind of things were so common that they eventually seemed like a score to a long, bad movie, entitled, "Tommy: the Franklin Saga."

The really memorable Marty pranks were a twisted combination of heartless sophistication and soul-less meanness. These events were often quite complex and were designed to unfold in front of others to achieve maximum humiliation.

**Mary-Ellen:** go on...

**Tommy:**  Imagine, if you will, the long tables in the middle school cafeteria.  Remember the pizza burgers on Fridays? I love them.  I also loved to pile on the Ketchup.

Unfortunately, Marty must have noticed that I often used about twice as much ketchup as any normal human being.  Apparently, he wanted to teach me a lesson about going easy on the ketchup.  Remember how the cafeteria ladies would set out the squeeze-able, plastic, ketchup bottles on the tables on Fridays?

**Mary-Ellen:** Yes.  I do remember that.  Mustard too. Right?

**Tommy:** Right.  Back to the story...
Anyway, Marty had gone through the lunch line ahead of me, and before I sat down he had loosened the lid of the ketchup bottle—just so.  You know what I mean?  Not enough to fall off until I squeezed it.  Then the lid shot off, in shot-gun-fashion on the burger, my plate, my tray, and a bit of my Eagles jersey.
Fun, huh?
You'd think I'd learn my lesson, right?  Not so fast. The very next week he got me again...even worse!
This time he had more time to plan.  This time he smuggled in a ketchup bottle that was the exact same type.  But in this one, loaded with ketchup, he had inserted a pencil's eraser in the nozzle.  It was nestled in there—just so.  Just enough to provoke an extra hard squeeze by me, the hapless victim.  Puzzled as to why

the ketchup was not coming out, I applied the extra-hard pressure in such a way that, when it exploded out the nozzle, it rocketed all over my pants. In the 'crotchal region', if you know what I mean?

**Mary-Ellen:** [unsuccessfully suppressing laugher] Yes.

**Tommy:** See. Even you have to laugh.

**Mary-Ellen:** Sorry, Tommy, but you tell it so well!

**Tommy:** I do, don't I. Now let me finish.
  My first reaction was to stand up and groan loudly...and, for some reason, direct everyone else's attention to the massive stream of dripping ketchup in the aforementioned 'crotchal region'.

**Mary-Ellen:** So, now everyone was laughing.

**Tommy:** You get the picture.

**Mary-Ellen:** What did you do? Did you play it up or run out of the room?

**Tommy:** I played it up, of course. I think I started laughing and muttering, "Oops, I sharted," over and over again as I walked, cowboy-style, out of the cafeteria to the bathroom.

**Mary-Ellen:** And you never told the principal who did this to you?

**Tommy:** Heck no. I'm lucky the teachers on caf duty didn't have their way. They wrote me up for "making a scene" and "making inappropriate, grotesque gestures" and the "use of crude language." Yes, the teacher who wrote me up made sure I headed to the principal's office the moment I walked out of the bathroom door...after cleaning my pants up.

**Mary-Ellen:** But you said you "were lucky the teachers didn't have their way?"

**Tommy:** Mrs. Turner, the middle school principal, had sympathy on me and didn't process the write-up. She let me off with a warning and told me to talk with Mrs. Bowers, the guidance counselor.

**Mary-Ellen:** Did you visit Mrs. Bowers.

**Tommy:** No way. She was like 24 years old...and a hot blonde. Do you really think I was about to saunter on down the hallway to her office and knock on her door...with a big, sticky-wet crotch blotch?

**Mary-Ellen:** I'm glad you can laugh about it now, looking back.

**Tommy:** Somehow I was able to laugh it off back then too. What else could I do? I wasn't gonna cry about it. Then Marty wins.

**Mary-Ellen:** That's an interesting way to look at it. That was pretty awful. Was that the worst of it in middle school?

**Tommy:** Unbelievably, no. You want to hear more?

**Mary-Ellen:** Definitely. I want more.

**Tommy:** All-righty-then...

Marty knew that I had a bad case of the sniffles in the spring when we were in 8th grade. I think it was in April when this happened.

The only way I could get through the day at school was to use nose spray a few times. I guess this annoyed Ty and Duwain and one of the girls was saying the "disgusting noises" I was making in the middle of class were "making her feel nauseous."

In those days we all carried nearly every book around with us so we wouldn't have to go to our lockers between classes and risk getting written up for being late. I had a zipper pouch on the front of my book bag. In the zipper pouch I kept the nose spray my mom bought for me. It was strong stuff and would really clear my sinuses. I don't remember the brand, but it was one of those "Fast Acting Nasal Sprays."

**Mary-Ellen:** So, did Marty threaten you to "Stop spraying and clearing your nose in class?"

**Tommy:** Not like that. He came up alongside of me in the hallway one day and whispered in my ear something like, "Hey...if you don't knock off the puking-out-the-nose sounds in class, I'm gonna stuff your nose up permanently." He did it all stealthy-like, with a smile on his smug face and everything.

**Mary-Ellen:** I take it that you didn't heed his warning.

**Tommy:** No, unfortunately I didn't. I used the stuff one day, toward the end of science class that week. I cleared my nose as quietly as I could, and then returned to my seat. I put the nasal spray in my pouch. Then the bell rang and we went to lunch. That class was divided into two parts.  The before lunch part was regular class.  The after-lunch part was a lab or activity.

**Mary-Ellen:**  Let me guess...
Did he put something in the nasal spray during lunch?

**Tommy:**  You're catching on.

**Mary-Ellen:**  Go on.

**Tommy:**  He slipped out of the caf with a pass to go to the restroom. Instead, he went back to the science room and went in my book bag.  He somehow switched my spray with a pre-rigged, nose spray container.

**Mary-Ellen:**  What did he put in it?

**Tommy:**  Patience...I'm getting there.
During 8$^{th}$ period that day, I was in another class when my nose was fully stuffed again.  I pulled out the spray and went to the back of the room, tilted my head back and sprayed it up both sides of my nose.  I held it in for a few seconds, like I usually do, and then grabbed a wad of Kleenex off the teacher's desk.  When I blew my nose tons of blood soaked the Kleenex and poured down my face.
I freaked out.  I mean I really freaked out.

**Mary-Ellen:**  You must have been scared.

**Tommy:**  I don't remember much about it.  I remember everyone looking at me like my head had just exploded. Before I fainted, I remember hearing Marty chuckling under his breath to Duwain,

"Dumbo's gonna bleed out. He uses that thing so much I think he punctured his brain with it."

I woke up in the nurse's office. She told me I had fainted and that there was nothing wrong with my nose. It was fake blood. The nasal spray container had fake blood in it!

**Mary-Ellen:** Tell me you nailed him. He got in trouble didn't he?

**Tommy:** Nope. Lots of people thought I had done it as a gag. Most people said stuff like, "Oh, Dumbo did it to get attention."

According to the principal, four kids told the teacher that I had told bragged about what I was planning on doing at lunch that day.

**Mary-Ellen:** Who told your teacher that?

**Tommy:** I know exactly who told, because Marty made fun of me on the bus on the way home, saying, "I hope you learned your lesson today, Dumbo. We told Mr. Diaz what you were braggin' about at lunchtime, stupid idiot."

**Mary-Ellen:** Ok, I don't know if I can take much more of this. Tell me one more...How 'bout one from high school?

**Tommy:** I'll skip to the end on these last two. The lead-in stories are long and boring.

Anyway, Marty's favorite trick was to undo the screws and bolts on desks and chairs. He knew how to make them collapse inward, so it would trap the victim between the desktop and the seat portion—like pincers. It hurt likc heck. As you can see, I'm a bit on the portly side, which was ideal for Marty and his jerkus friends because they could always get a lot of hideous people to laugh at my pain as I lay on the floor struggling to work my way loose from the heap.

His second favorite practical joke was to have someone else write a note about me, or some of the other less popular kids, and drop it in the "Comments and Concerns Box" outside of the guidance office.

**Mary-Ellen:** Really? Hum, this sounds familiar. Were these notes about you signed by anyone? Or were they the handiwork of some nameless, 'concerned citizen?'

**Tommy:** The 'nameless, concerned friend.'

**Mary-Ellen:** What type of concerns did your friend reveal about you?

**Tommy:** Serious stuff. It got me in serious trouble.

**Mrs. Tombeaux:** Very serious. I think they were trying to get Tommy expelled.

**Mary-Ellen:** Did any of these notes from your 'concerned friend' reveal that you were using drugs?

**Mrs. Tombeaux:** Yes. Tommy's lucky that I knew better. My boy may be many things, but I knew he wasn't using or dealing ecstasy.

**Mary-Ellen:** Tommy, it was just the word of a nameless person. You couldn't get in trouble for that. You didn't, did you?

**Tommy:** No.  But after several failed attempts on their part, I think Marty took it to the next level.

**Mary-Ellen:** How so?

**Tommy:** One of the notes indicated that I had "x" in my school locker.  When the vice-principal did a check, he found some on top of a pile of old notebooks.  I was taken out of the school in hand cuffs...in front of everyone.

[At this point, the interview ended.  Tommy could not go on.]

# Mr. Carl Denker

The following is the transcript of my interview with Mr. Carl Denker, conducted in the guidance office, suite B, of Franklin High School, Jedesdorf, PA.

Date: June 20, 2011
Time: 3:47-4:25 PM


**Mary-Ellen:** Mr. Denker, please tell me about your educational background and experience in education.

**Mr. Denker:** I've been a school psychologist and guidance councilor for 5 years at Franklin High School. I hold a bachelor's degree from Drexel University and a master's from Lehigh University.

**Mary-Ellen:** Do you enjoy your work?

**Mr. Denker:** Immensely. It's a tough job sometimes, but it's rewarding when you can make a difference in the lives of students.

**Mary-Ellen:** I really appreciate your efforts in helping me out with other interviews, particularly your help securing an interview with Officer Street.

**Mr. Denker:** No problem. Officer Street is a personal friend. I've known him for ten years.

**Mary-Ellen:** OK. The first thing I want to know about is Ashley's depression. Ashley's parents told me that their son was diagnosed with depression a few

years ago and that you knew about it.  I have a letter
from them if you'd like to see it.  They give you
permission to discuss the matter and anything else you
know about him that may be related to his death.

**Mr. Denker:**  Yes.  Normally discussing a subject like
Ashley's mental state is a privacy issue.  I've talked with
Mr. and Mrs. White on several occasions and they've
made it abundantly clear that I may share the
information with you.

I've known about Ashley White's mild depression
for three years.  He was on a low dosage of Prozac
from his freshman year until January of his junior year
at Franklin.

**Mary-Ellen:**  Why do you think he was depressed?

**Mr. Denker:**  Ashley had unrealistic concerns about
having acne. He told me that he had been mercilessly
teased by some of the popular kids back in 8th grade.
When he was in middle school his parents took him to
Dr. Bosh, their family doctor.  Dr. Bosh prescribed an
antidepressant as well as an acne med called Accutane.
It cleared up the acne completely—and very quickly,
from what I remember.  I can't recall Ashley having a
single pimple in 9th grade.  I don't think he even had
any noticeable acne scars. Still, Ashley was scarred
inside. We talked on numerous occasions and his self-
esteem had been deeply wounded.

**Mary-Ellen:**  Did he ever mention which kids were
teasing him?

**Mr. Denker:**  He never wanted to share that
information.  He had a real aversion to being a

"snitch". Truth is, I knew the likely candidates from the complaints of a dozen other students who were also treated like dirt by the same kids.

**Mary-Ellen:** What names came up time and time again in this respect?

**Mr. Denker:** Brenda Waxman, among the girls in Ashley's class, was—*by far*—the worst offender. Among the boys, there are several: Joey Prepotente, Duwain Williams, and Marty Fine.

**Mary-Ellen:** Among the people you've just named, did you ever have any reason to believe that they might be involved in drugs.

**Mr. Denker:** Yes. I was made aware of student use of the drug ecstasy by way of a note and private conversation with Trudy Schroeder. She left a note in my Student Concerns Box. It's a drop box that students can use to anonymously express concerns and give me a heads up about things that are going on in school that shouldn't be without their friends knowing they were the source.

**Mary-Ellen:** When did she leave the note?

**Mr. Denker:** It was in February—last year. Trudy was in Ashley's class.

**Mary-Ellen:** I've heard a bunch about this letter. I've seen a copy of it. Do you have the original?

**Mr. Denker:** I saved the letter. I still have it in her file. When Trudy came to my office that day in March she admitted to trying the drug at parties and was concerned with the side effects. She refused to tell me who was peddling the drugs, but she did tell me the drugs were distributed at several of Marty Fine's parties. I convinced her to stop taking the drug.

**Mary-Ellen:** Are you aware that Trudy denies sending you the note? She denies ever meeting with you in private. I don't know how else to say this, but, are you aware that she claims that she would never allow herself to be alone in a room with you because she claims you ogle all the "hot girls" at Franklin?

**Mr. Denker:** Ogle? That's slander. Why would she say something like that? Unbelievable!

**Mary-Ellen:** Duwain Williams told me the same thing. He made it sound like every pretty girl in the school made it a point to stay away from you because you were looking at them inappropriately.

**Mr. Denker:** Hold on. You know which girls are considered attractive at Franklin. Let me show you something.

This is my appointment book. Look at these names from this past month. Heck, look at some of these names from around the time that Trudy came into my office. Here…here's her name——she came in here three times in March of last year. Look at these other names. Wouldn't you admit that many of these girls are thought to be attractive by other students?

**Mary-Ellen:** Um…yeah. Definitely.

**Mr. Denker:** *These* girls weren't afraid of me 'ogling' them or being 'inappropriate with them in private.' There's at least 7 here that are just as pretty as Trudy.

**Mary-Ellen:** Great point, Mr. Denker. I'm Sorry I even had to bring that up. Please don't think I believe that about you.

OK. Let's talk about what happened on Monday, May 13, when Ashley ran out of Ms. Lehrer's class and ended up in your office.

**Mr. Denker:** Around 1:00 in the afternoon the nurse brought Ashley White into my office. He was crying and was holding a cold compress on his forehead. At first he seemed completely out of it. But after he calmed down I talked with him about what had happened. Ashley admitted he had a crush on Mary Margaret Dolce, and that he had been leaving her quite a few love notes over several months. He said he kept doing it because she seemed to be so happy with them. He told me that leaving the notes and seeing how happy it made her gave him new self-confidence. He knew Mary Margaret had discovered it was him. He told me that someone had posted one of his "most personal" and "sappy" love poems to M&M on a poster in Ms. Lehrer's class in order to embarrass him.

**Mary-Ellen:** Did he tell you who did that to him?

**Mr. Denker:** He had no idea. But with Brenda and Marty in that class he was certain that the whole school would be hearing about the embarrassment he had just suffered.

**Mary-Ellen:** Why did Ashley storm out of the building?  It sounds like you're saying he was calming down.

**Mr. Denker:** Around 2:15 in the afternoon his mood changed and he started to get irritated, agitated, angry...and then extremely fidgety.  It seemed like he was having an anxiety attack.  He started repeating the same thing over and over again:  "I'm finished with this #@*K- -- g place.  I hate this #@*K- -- g place.  I'm ruined.  I'll never be able to show my face again.  I'm outta here and never coming back!"

Ashley's eyes were wild with anxiety and he attempted to run out of the office past me.  I tried to stop him from leaving. I stood in the doorway. I stood in his way.  So did the principal.  Dr. Gallman had overheard the yelling—he's the next room over—and he came over to my office.  But there were only a few minutes left in the school day...plus, Ashley was 18 years old and was warning us to "keep our hands off of him" and that, "We had no right to stop an adult from leaving school!"

**Mary-Ellen:** Sounds like it was pretty intense.  Was Ashley within his rights to leave?  Was he right about that?

**Mr. Denker:** Technically, he was correct.  We had no right to stop him from leaving the building. Still, Dr. Gallman and I had to consider his personal safety while he was on school property, and the safety of other students.

**Mary-Ellen:** Where you concerned that Ashley might flip out on other students in the hallway or lobby or in the parking lot?

**Mr. Denker:** Yes. We were concerned about how he might react to being confronted by other students as the bell rang for dismissal.

For that reason alone, I think Dr. Gallman made the right call. He kept calm and guided Ashley out of the building...knowing Ashley might 'flip out' as you put it.

**Mary-Ellen:** What did you do next...after he left?

**Mr. Denker:** We tried to contact Ashley's parents, but couldn't reach them at home or at work. We found out later that they were on vacation for their twentieth wedding anniversary. They were in the Bahamas.

**Mary-Ellen:** Did you notify the local police?

**Mr. Denker:** I didn't. Dr. Gallman did. He had his secretary look up Ashley's files quickly, so he could give a description of Ashley's vehicle and license plate number.

**Mary-Ellen:** As far as you or Dr. Gallman knew, were the police sending out a squad car or cars to look for Ashley?

**Mr. Denker:** The police asked Dr. Gallman whether a crime had been committed by Ashley. Since Ashley had not broken any law, the only thing the police were willing to do was to send over two officers to monitor the parking lot/entrance/exit area of the high school.

**Mary-Ellen:** So, as far as you two knew, the police did not actively pursue or look for Ashley?

**Mr. Denker:** That's correct. They did not actively pursue, try to intercept, or hunt him down. They did, however, put out an all points bulletin to the other patrolmen in the county, and, I think, the State Police too. In other words, the police knew about the situation. They had orders to be on the lookout for Ashley's vehicle—in case he was driving erratically or was breaking the law in some other way.

**Mary-Ellen:** Now, you're talking about the police not being able to do anything unless Ashley was breaking the law. Right?

**Mr. Denker:** Right.

**Mary-Ellen:** Well, it seems to me that you...or should I say *they*...were referring to establishing "probable cause". I mean, without probable cause, they can't just pull Ashley—*or anyone else*—over. Right?

**Mr. Denker:** That's correct. That's the way the police saw the matter. They never used that terminology, though.

**Mary-Ellen:** Well, now looking back at the way Ashley was behaving in your office on Monday, May 13, do you think it was possible that he was on drugs...or had been drugged?

**Mr. Denker:** It *did* cross our minds. You know that. You and I have talked about this before...more than a few times. Now, considering what may have happened at lunch that same day...considering that a drug may have been slipped into Ashley's chocolate milk...

**Mary-Ellen:** Sorry to interrupt, Mr. Denker...So, based on what you and Dr. Gallman witnessed— *Ashley's possibly drugged, erratic behavior*—wouldn't that be probable cause enough to detain him at school? Additionally, why didn't the police consider your report of a possibly drugged student driving off of campus during a busy traffic time to be probable cause to intercept and detain Ashley...for his own safety and the safety of others? I don't get it.

**Mr. Denker:** It was a judgment call on our part. We had to balance Ashley's rights with the *possibility* he was on drugs. We had no *proof* he was on drugs when he left school, and neither did the police.

**Mary-Ellen:** OK, I find that answer very frustrating. That's all for now. Thanks for consenting to the interview.

**Mr. Denker:** You're welcome. Good luck with what you're doing here. I'm with you, one-hundred percent.

**Mary-Ellen:** Thanks.

[As Mr. Denker leaves suite B, Dr. Gallman arrives]

## Lee Gallman, Ed. D.

The following is the transcript of my interview with Dr. Lee Gallman, conducted in the guidance office, suite B, of Franklin High School, Jedesdorf, PA.

Date: June 20, 2011
Time: 4:25-5:00 PM

**Dr. Gallman:** Am I on time?

**Mary-Ellen:** Right on time.

**Dr. Gallman:** Is an hour good enough? I have to be out of here by 5:30.

**Mary-Ellen:** That's plenty of time. I don't have too many questions for you.

**Dr. Gallman:** Well then, let's get down to business.

**Mary-Ellen:** Thinking back to Monday, May 13...what do you remember about Ashley White's mental state and physical demeanor when you and the nurse corralled him in the main lobby?

**Dr. Gallman:** He was nearly beside himself with rage. He was cursing. I had known Ashley to be such a gentle spirit, to hear him yell and curse was...well, shocking.

**Mary-Ellen:** So, his cursing was way out of the norm?

**Dr. Gallman:** It was completely out of the norm for Ashley White.

**Mary-Ellen:** Did you wonder whether Ashley might be high?

**Dr. Gallman:** That only crossed my mind later. At the time, I assumed his words and actions were the result of rage. Although not everything he said made sense, I understood the gist of it. He was upset by a nasty practical joke. He kept repeating the same story. I'm paraphrasing, of course, but he continually yelled about "Marty making a blankety-blank fool out of me!"; that "Blanking Marty embarrassed me in front of everyone!"; that Blanking blankety-blank set me up!"; that "I'm never going to be able to show my blanking face in this blankety-blank place again...I'm leaving!"

**Mary-Ellen:** How did you get Ashley to calm down and to go to guidance?

**Dr. Gallman:** I told him I'd look into the matter. I assured him that Marty would be held accountable. I told Ashley that he'd have to explain what happened first, that way I'd know how to handle Marty Fine. I told Ashley I'd get to the bottom of what happened to him, with the help of the local police if necessary.

**Mary-Ellen:** Was Mr. Denker helpful in this regard? And the nurse?

**Dr. Gallman:** Very helpful. Ashley trusted Mr. Denker, and Mr. Denker had apparently spoken with Ashley about a variety of issues over a few years.

The nurse was primarily concerned with Ashley's physical health and safety...appropriately so. She attempted to coax Ashley to come to the health suite, but he would have none of it. He flat-out refused to go. He did, however, allow her to apply a cold compress to his head. Well, she gave it to him and Ashley held it to his own head.

**Mary-Ellen:** Did the nurse check Ashley's eyes for signs of a concussion?

**Dr. Gallman:** She tried. Ashley resisted her attempt to shine a light at his pupils to check their re-activity. He told her to "Get out of my face!" and would have pushed her away if Mr. Denker had not stood between them.

I told her to stand-by outside of Denker's office and that we'd call her if we needed her.

**Mary-Ellen:** Do you think Ashley may have had a concussion? Did you have a chance to look at his eyes?

**Dr. Gallman:** Not his eyes. The welt on the side of his forehead...I saw that. It was large and looked like it hurt quite a bit. He was obviously in physical pain. His posture was angular and closed and he grimaced with pain that was clearly as much physical as it was emotional.

**Mary-Ellen:** I want to skip forward in time a bit because I know Ashley and Mr. Denker were behind closed doors for a few minutes.

**Dr. Gallman:** That's true.

**Mary-Ellen:** When Ashley had, for lack of a better description, a second fit of rage and ran out of the building, what was the first thing you did?

**Dr. Gallman:** I called the local police.

**Mary-Ellen:** Mr. Denker told me that the police didn't feel they had "probable cause" to find/hunt down Ashley and detain him. Is that accurate?

**Dr. Gallman:** Yes. That's accurate.

**Mary-Ellen:** I'm curious. Did you wonder or did the police wonder whether Ashley was a danger to himself, considering his state of mind and nasty head injury?

**Dr. Gallman:** Yes, we were all concerned with that. I mean, behind the wheel he was a potential danger to others too.

**Mary-Ellen:** So, would you consider his state of mind to be "probable cause" if you had been an officer?

**Dr. Gallman:** Yes, but I'm not sure it actually is—in a strictly legal sense. The police, and law outside of these grounds arc(indicating with his hands that he was referring to the school district property), well, different. There are different standards for probable cause in different jurisdictions.

**Mary-Ellen:** Yes, or so I've been told.
  Moving on...
  I know form Mr. Denker and a brief conversation with Mrs. Brown, your secretary, that you all tried desperately to contact Ashley White's parents. Do you

think you did everything you could have done to get
reach them?

**Dr. Gallman**:  Everything.

**Mary-Ellen:**  Do you or your secretary have record of
these attempts.

**Dr. Gallman:**  Yes, and copies of those documents
were forwarded to the District Attorney's Office last
June.

**Mary-Ellen:**  Yes, I know.
   Now, one more question and then we're done.

**Dr. Gallman:**  Fire away.

**Mary-Ellen:**  In your personal opinion, having sat in
on so many interviews with the students involved in
this case, do you hold Marty Fine responsible for
Ashley White's death.

**Dr. Gallman:**  Well, I don't like to play the role of
judge and jury.  And in this case it looks like there will
never be a judge or jury.

**Mary-Ellen:**  Sir...I understand that. I just want to
know.  Do you think I'm crazy for believing Marty
Fine, and probably a few others, should be in jail for
some form of homicide?

**Dr. Gallman:**  Now, this is not a legal opinion, I'm not
a lawyer...let me be clear.  But, if given the chance to
testify in criminal court, I would feel compelled to say
Marty should be held responsible for what happened.

He wasn't directly responsible, but he—and you're right, probably his friends—were the indirect cause of Ashley's crash.

**Mary-Ellen:**  If they were the indirect cause of the crash, weren't they also the indirect cause of his death?

**Dr. Gallman:**  I would say so.  You're not crazy, Mary-Ellen.  But you're like a bulldog out for justice.  You're like no kid I've ever had in all my years in education.
   Mary-Ellen, I'm very proud of you.  How many teenage girls care this deeply about what they perceive to me as miscarriage of justice?  Heck, most of the adults involved in this case have already moved on.

**Mary-Ellen:**  Thank you, Dr. Gallman, you have no idea how good it makes me feel to hear someone say I'm not crazy and all.

[At this point the interview ended because I wanted to go home and cry in private]

## Deena Fawks

The following is the transcript of my interview with
Deena Fawks, conducted in the guidance office of
Franklin High School, Jedesdorf, PA.

Date:  June 21, 2011
Time:  2:40-3:09 PM
Witness:  Mr. Roger D. Flory (Teacher).


**Mary-Ellen:**  Tell me about your background and
professional qualifications.

**Ms. Fawks:**  I graduated from Franklin High School a
few years back.  Then I successfully completed The
City University of Philadelphia's Associate of Applied
Science in EMT-Paramedic program two years ago.
That's the highest degree one can attain for my field.
Before that, I had experience in the US Navy as a field
medic.

**Mary-Ellen:**  Is it true that you're related to M&M,
and that you were the first medical professional to
arrive at Ashley's accident?

**Ms. Fawks:**  Mary Margaret Dolce is my cousin.  Her
dad's sister is my aunt.  Yes, I was the first responders
at the accident scene.

**Mary-Ellen:**  Would you mind describing your
duties/responsibilities as a first responder?

**Ms. Fawks:** It is my job to provide out-of-hospital acute care and transport to definitive care, to patients with illnesses and injuries which the patient—if they are aware of the situation—or I believe constitutes a medical emergency.

**Mary-Ellen:** When did you get the call?

**Ms. Fawks:** I was called to the scene of a single car accident by the 9-1-1 dispatcher. The severe accident was along Rt. 429, heading west of Franklin. I arrived at the crash site at approximately 4:21 PM.

**Mary-Ellen:** What condition was Ashley in when you arrived?

**Ms. Fawks:** When I arrived, on-scene, the victim was dead and could not be revived.

**Mary-Ellen:** Could Mr. Thomas have done anything, prior to your arrival, to help save Ashley's life?

**Ms. Fawks:** In my expert opinion, the jogger, Frank Thomas, couldn't have done anything to save the victim. He did what he should have: he called 9-1-1 right away, less than a minute after witnessing the accident.

**Mary-Ellen:** Is it true that you looked around Ashley's car with Officer Street afterwards to see what might explain the crash?

**Ms. Fawks:** Yes.

**Mary-Ellen:** Did you find anything of interest?

**Ms. Fawks:**  I found an empty package of Accutane in the glove compartment of the Dodge Daytona.  We turned the contents of the vehicle over to the County Coroner's Office.

**Mary-Ellen:**  Where you looking for anything in particular?

**Ms. Fawks:**  Yes.  I didn't know who the deceased was, so I looked for ID on the body but was unable to find any.  That's why I looked in the glove compartment.  I was looking for ID of any sort, but there wasn't any.  No wallet.  No driver's license.  No school ID.

**Mary-Ellen:**  After you found out who had died, did you call M&M?

**Ms. Fawks:**  That night when I found out from the Coroner that it was a Franklin HS student, I called my younger cousin, Mary Margaret Dolce.  When she found out who had died, she was devastated and told me about the love notes Ashley White had been giving her.  She was convinced he had committed suicide and felt responsible.  I told her to call the police and talk to Officer Street about the love notes, etc.  She promised me she would, and she did.  Officer Street is a very close friend of mine and he confirmed that he had spoken with Mary Margaret.  He spoke with a number of students at Franklin and quickly became convinced that something more than suicide had happened, and that illegal activities at school may have resulted in Ashley White's death.  You should talk to the County Coroner's Office about the autopsy.  When Officer

Street did, he became convinced that something criminal had taken place.

## Robert Benjamin, PI

The following is the transcript of my interview with Robert Benjamin, conducted in the guidance office of Franklin High School, Jedesdorf, PA.

Date: June 21, 2011
Time: 3:30-4:20 PM


**Mary-Ellen:** What do you do for a living, sir?

**Mr. Benjamin:** I'm a private investigator and owner of Pinnacle Investigations in Nathan's Creek, PA.

**Mary-Ellen:** What is your educational background?

**Mr. Benjamin:** I went to Muhlenberg College for my BA. I majored in criminal justice, criminology and investigative studies at Temple University for my Masters degree. I worked for an investigative firm in New Jersey for five years before striking out on my own.

**Mary-Ellen:** How did you get involved in the Ashley White case?

**Mr. Benjamin:** Ashley White's parents contacted me on the morning of Tuesday, May 14. They called from Nassau in the Bahamas because they'd received phone calls from the school psychologist, Mr. Denker and Officer Street earlier that morning. Mr. and Mrs. White were stunned. They couldn't believe their son was dead. They were in the airport catching the first available flight to Philly, when they connected the dots. They put together what Mr. Denker had told them about Ashley's uncharacteristically bizarre behavior and sudden departure from school at the end of the day on May 13 and info about the prank that some student or students had played on him in Ms. Lehrer's class and his death by reckless driving. They just couldn't accept that Ashley had been driving recklessly. They couldn't believe he had taken drugs willingly. The whole story felt like it had gaping holes in it. They hired me to supplement the investigation launched by Officer Street.

**Mary-Ellen:** Based on your investigation, should the DA have filed charges against any of the students?

**Mr. Benjamin:** Yes. Their worry was *proving* their case. The case would have been a circumstantial one. It would have been very difficult to prove a case against Marty Fine. The jury would have had to come to a unanimous conclusion that Marty had intentionally drugged and created a grossly negligent situation by way of the classroom prank. The DA would have had to prove beyond a reasonable doubt that Ashley's crash and death were caused by Marty's criminal negligence or recklessness. They would have had to prove that Marty was responsible without much solid evidence.

**Mary-Ellen:** If the DA could prove to the jury that Marty spiked the chocolate milk and that Ashley drove away from the school that day higher than a kite, wouldn't Marty be charged with first degree murder?

**Mr. Benjamin:** No. Proving he spiked the drink still wouldn't prove Marty intended for Ashley to get physically hurt, let alone intending Ashley to die.

**Mary-Ellen:** I can't imagine anyone in their right mind believing that Marty and his helpers didn't intend for Ashley to get hurt. They set up the chair and loosened the screws.

**Mr. Benjamin:** True. I think it would have been be quite easy to prove Marty and his co-conspirators intended to embarrass. Proving they intended for Ashley to get *physically hurt* would have been problematic. Proving Marty wanted for Ashley to get a concussion by setting up the prank would have been very difficult.

**Mary-Ellen:** Proving that they should have known that they were recklessly endangering Ashley—and potentially others in the classroom—should have been easy. Right?

**Mr. Benjamin:** *Easier.* Not easy. The DA would still have to prove beyond a reasonable doubt that Marty and his co-conspirators should have foreseen the potential and serious consequences of their prank.

**Mary-Ellen:** Sounds to me like any jury with common sense could be shown that Marty and his helpers should have known they were doing something that might seriously injure Ashley.

**Mr. Benjamin:** I think you're correct. The key would be to connect prior pranks to this one. For example, in my investigation I found out from several people I interrogated that Marty had physically hurt a teacher during his 8th grade year. The poor guy broke his coccyx. The same prank was used in both cases.

**Mary-Ellen:** What would the DA have charged Marty with if they had prosecuted him for the sort of criminal recklessness where he should have known better based on prior experience where his prank went too far and hurt someone seriously?

**Mr. Benjamin:** Do you understand that the charge you're describing wouldn't even involve Ashley's death?

**Mary-Ellen:** I suppose it wouldn't. That just doesn't seem fair to separate the two events like that. After all, who would believe that Ashley would have driven out of school that day, high as a kite, crashed his car and died without the prank? Without the prank Ashley would still be alive. It seems like a chain of events that can't be separated like that.

**Mr. Benjamin:** It *seems* that way. But imagine how difficult it would be for the District Attorney to *prove beyond a reasonable doubt* that the Marty's criminal negligence was the cause of Ashley's reckless driving and crash. Any good defense attorney would have been able to cast significant doubt on the situation. They would say things like, "Ashley was embarrassed in front of his class, had somehow self-medicated by ingesting ecstasy, and then crashed." The DA would have to *prove* that Marty put the ecstasy in the chocolate milk.

**Mary-Ellen:** They have an eyewitness. Mercedes Perez saw Marty put the chocolate milk with the sticky note on Ashley's table!

**Mr. Benjamin:** That's one witness. There were others who contradicted Mercedes and the defense would call them to the stand to testify. There were even people who told me that Mercedes put the chocolate milk on the table.

**Mary-Ellen:** Then it comes down to proving which witnesses are liars. Proving which ones are reliable, truthful...believable.

**Mr. Benjamin:** Sounds easy, but it's not. I don't mean to put a damper on your theory here. *I'm with you.* Marty and a few others are responsible for Ashley's death. Mercedes is telling the truth and the others who contradict her and have attempted to indict her are *liars.* About that, I have no doubt.

But our problem in *proving* this theory to 12 jurors goes even deeper. Let's say the DA *can* prove that Marty put the chocolate milk on Ashley's table. Now does that *necessarily* mean that Marty spiked it with ecstasy? Does his placement of the milk on the table prove anything more than...he put milk on Ashley's table?

**Mary-Ellen:** My head is about to explode. This is soooo...arghhh....

**Mr. Benjamin:** I understand your frustration.

**Mary-Ellen:**  But can't we prove that Marty was dealing ecstasy and therefore was the most likely person to spike the milk?

**Mr. Benjamin:**  Most likely, yes—absolute proof, no. For example, what if one of the girls—like Brenda or Trudy or even M&M had saved one of the pills from the party on Saturday night.  What if one of them had decided to spice up the prank by spiking the chocolate milk?

**Mary-Ellen:**  If **they** did it, **they** would have told Marty.  To me, that just means that **they** should *all* be charged as co-conspirators to commit criminally negligent homicide.

**Mr. Benjamin:**  Good luck.  I hope you find something that re-invigorates the DA's desire to prosecute this case.  If you need any specific information from me, just give me a call.

**Mary-Ellen:**  Thanks, Mr. Benjamin, I will.

## Sgt. Corrine Street

The following is the transcript of my interview with Sgt. Corrine Street, conducted in the guidance office of Franklin High School, Jedesdorf, PA.

Date: June 24, 2011
Time: 2:40-3:13 PM

**Mary-Ellen:** Officer Street, how old are you? And how many years experience do you have as a detective?

**Officer Street:** I'm 27 years old. This is my first full year as a detective in Upper Adams Township, Franklin County.

**Mary-Ellen:** How did you become involved in the Ashley White case?

**Officer Street:** I was called to the scene of a fatal accident by the 9-1-1 dispatcher on the afternoon of Monday, May 13. I arrived at the crash site at 4:35, just as the EMS team had declared Ashley White dead. It was my job to file an accident report. I wrote the accident report.

**Mary-Ellen:** Beyond this just being an accident. When and how did you become involved in a criminal investigation?

**Officer Street:** I was contacted the next morning by private investigator Benjamin. He had been hired by the White family to conduct an investigation at

Franklin High School and beyond.  PI Benjamin informed me that the school psychologist, Mr. Denker, had contacted the family too.  Mr. Denker had provided us with information about a possible drug connection.  Since the autopsy turned up ecstasy in Ashley White's system, things were looking mighty suspicious.

**Mary-Ellen:**  Tell me more about Mr. Denker's conversation with the White family.

**Officer Street:**  On the morning of May 14, Denker had called Ashley's parents about the prank that had been pulled on their son in Ms. Lehrer's class.  Believe it or not, when he called Mr. and Mrs. White, he wasn't aware of Ashley's crash and death.  So, when I called the Whites in Nassau they thought I had the wrong victim.  They couldn't believe it.  They had just talked with Mr. Denker about the in-school incident that had taken place on the 13th of May.

**Mary-Ellen:**  You conducted interviews of students and teachers and administrators as Franklin.  Correct?

**Officer Street:**  Correct.  I conducted several interrogations of students at Franklin.  Some of the students called parents first before they were interrogated, some even called lawyers.  Every student was Mirandized.

**Mary-Ellen:**  The initial investigations took place on Tuesday, May 14.  Correct?

**Officer Street:**  Yes.  They lasted most of the school day.  Most students waived their right to have a lawyer present during the interrogation.  However, Marty Fine, Brenda Waxman and Ty Weiser's parents brought in a lawyer.  At the end of the school day, I arrested Marty Fine and booked him for felony drugging and reckless endangerment of a fellow student.  Several other students' parents were told to remain in-state until further notice and that they faced potential criminal conspiracy charges.

I consulted with the Franklin County District Attorney before the arrest.  The DA filed charges of involuntary manslaughter and reckless endangerment against Martin Fine that very same day and Marty had his first appearance in front of the judge late that afternoon.

**Mary-Ellen:** Reckless endangerment?  Explain this, please.

**Officer Street:** Recklessness of a criminal nature usually arises when the accused is aware of the potentially adverse consequences to the planned actions, but has gone ahead anyway, exposing a particular individual or unknown victim to the risk of suffering the foreseen harm but not actually desiring that the victim be hurt. The accused is deemed a "danger to society" because they've gambled with the safety of another.  The fact that Marty might have acted to try to avoid the injury from occurring is relevant only to mitigate the sentence—if found guilty.

**Mary-Ellen:** I've heard that the phrase "gross criminal negligence" might have applied to this case.  Is that true?

**Officer Street:** Gross criminal negligence represents a *serious* failure to foresee that in any other person, it would have been recklessness. In other words, that Marty deliberately engineered a situation in which he ignored material facts, or that the failure to foresee represented such a danger to others that it must be treated as though it was extremely reckless.

**Mary-Ellen:** Could this charge have applied to Marty?

**Officer Street:** We thought so. Let me read the definition to make things more clear: "Gross criminal negligence involves conduct whereby the actor does not desire harmful consequence but...foresees the possibility and consciously takes the risk." In common language this charge applies to a state of mind in which a person does not care about the harmful and potentially hurtful and dangerous consequences.

**Mary-Ellen:** Sounds exactly like what I think Marty did to Ashley. But I think his recklessness is responsible for Ashley's death. It doesn't sound like Marty was ever charged with criminally negligent homicide. It sounds like homicide was not a charge here.

**Officer Street:** That's because it wasn't.

**Mary-Ellen:** Why not? Certainly your interrogations turned up the fact that Marty spiked Ashley's...

**Officer Street:** Yes, I know where you're going with this. In my investigation and interviews with other students I found out that Marty Fine may have spiked Ashley White's chocolate milk with the drug Ecstasy during lunch that day.  That's why he was charged with felony drugging.

**Mary-Ellen:**  What information or evidence was essential to the decision to go with this charge?

**Officer Street:**  I spoke at length with Paisley Wahr about the note from Mary Margaret that Ashley received at lunchtime on Monday, May 13.  Paisley told me about the half-pint-sized carton of chocolate milk and a yellow sticky note with a "Thank you message" from Mary Margaret Dolce.

Our problem was we could never track down the carton and note.  We went through a mountain of trash at the school and never found it.  We know what kind of container it was, what it looked like, and what the sticky note said—*approximately, that is*.  We had to depend on Paisley's memory for what the note from Mary Margaret Dolce actually said.

**Mary-Ellen:**  Did you check Ashley White's locker and car?

**Officer Street:**  Yes.  No carton or note.

**Mary-Ellen:**  Did you check other lockers or personal belongings of the students potentially involved in the prank?

**Officer Street:**  Unfortunately, no.

**Mary-Ellen:**  Did you investigate whether or not any of the lunch ladies or maintenance workers at Franklin High might have seen someone rooting through the trash or dumpsters?

## Officer Street: No.

# Dr. Kevin Todt, M.D., Medical Examiner & County Coroner

The following is the transcript of my interview with Dr. Kevin Todt, conducted in the guidance office of Franklin High School, Jedesdorf, PA.

Date: June 24, 2011
Time: 4:00-4:42 PM

**Mary-Ellen:** First off, I want to thank you so much for taking time out of your busy schedule.

**Dr. Todt:** I feel it is my duty. I'm impressed by your desire to educate yourself. Perhaps you should pursue criminology, law or even forensic studies in college.

**Mary-Ellen:** I appreciate the compliment. It's journalism for me. I want to specialize in criminal reporting.

Dr. Todt, would you please review your educational background?

**Dr. Todt:** I hold a Doctor of Osteopathic Medicine (D.O.) from University of Pennsylvania Medical School. I went on to complete my education at the University of Wisconsin at Madison, achieving board certification as a forensic pathologist [1] after 4 years in the program.

**Mary-Ellen:** What is your current profession?

**Dr. Todt:** I am the Franklin County Coroner [2].

**Mary-Ellen:** That makes you an expert on determining the cause of death.  Correct?

**Dr. Todt:** Yes.

**Mary-Ellen:** Did you speak with Mr. Denker regarding the use of ecstasy at my school?

**Dr. Todt:** Yes, I spoke with the school psychologist about student use of ecstasy at Franklin High School after finding the drug in Ashley White's system.

**Mary-Ellen:** Would you mind giving some details about the drug and its effects?

**Dr. Todt:** When I did the autopsy [3] I found Methylenedioxymethamphetamine, MDMA [4] for short, in Ashley White's bloodstream.  MDMA is known by the street name "Ecstasy."

Taken orally, MDMA usually noticeably takes effect in about 30-45 minutes. Though, in some cases, a person can start to feel high in as little as 20 minutes. The onset of symptoms depends a lot on dosage, an individual's metabolism [5], if it was taken with food and how much food. First time users many times take around an hour for the effects to kick in, especially if the person is feeling anxiety about the possible dangers or actively fighting the feelings.  This delay for first time users leads to people overdosing because they think the absence of immediate effects means they didn't take enough to "feel it".

**Mary-Ellen:** When would a person taking a single pill feel the most high?

**Dr. Todt:**  Peak effects could be felt anywhere from 60 to 90 minutes after taking MDMA.

**Mary-Ellen:**  How is ecstasy usually taken?

**Dr. Todt:**  "E" or "X" is almost always swallowed as a tablet or capsule, but it can come in liquid form. A normal dose is around 100-125 mg.  Black market [6]ecstasy tablets vary widely in strength, and often contain other drugs.

**Mary-Ellen:**  Do the pills dissolve in liquid?  And will a dissolved pill in liquid take effect more quickly?

**Dr. Todt:**  A crushed pill will dissolve more quickly than a whole pill, causing a more rapid, stronger onset. Dissolving the pill would take a while, but crushing it up and shaking it or stirring it into a liquid would take only a few seconds.   I know what you're driving at. You're thinking that someone crushed up a pill and mixed it into the chocolate milk that Ashley White ingested [7] at lunch on the day of his death.

**Mary-Ellen:**  Yes.  I imagine that's how it happened.

**Dr. Todt:**  I had the same thought from the very start. However, something has always bothered me.  The District Attorney's Office also found it a major sticking point.  MDMA has a noticeably bitter taste, even when dissolved in a sugary drink like chocolate milk.  It's hard for me to imagine that Ashley didn't notice. Certainly he would have noticed the odd, bitter taste.

**Mary-Ellen:** Paisley Wahr remembers Ashley remarking that the chocolate milk tasted bitter. So, to me, that makes sense. Did you find anything else in Ashley's system?

**Dr. Todt:** I found Fluoxetine Hydrochloride [8] in Ashley's blood. FH is more commonly called Prozac. Prozac is an antidepressant [9]. Normally prescribed amounts were found in his system. He had not taken more than what the doctor had prescribed.

**Mary-Ellen:** What are the side effects of FH?

**Dr. Todt:** Among the common adverse effects associated with FH are nausea (22%), insomnia [10] (19%), somnolence [11](12%), anorexia [12] (10%), anxiety (12%), nervousness (13%), asthenia [13](11%), and tremors [14](9%).

**Mary-Ellen:** What about side effects caused by mixing FH with MDMA?

**Dr. Todt:** When mixed with MDMA, the most likely side effects would be extreme anxiety, nervousness and even panic-attacks.

**Mary-Ellen:** That sounds similar to what those who witnessed Ashley's behavior after his fall in English class. It makes perfect sense. His behavior matched what you are saying would be the side effects of ingestion of both drugs.

According to Deena Fawks, the EMT [15] at the scene of the accident, Ashley had the drug Accutane [16] in his glove compartment. Do you think this drug was part of the reason Ashley seemed to go crazy?

**Dr. Todt:** The police informed me of an empty package of the prescription acne drug, Accutane, found in the glove compartment of Ashley White's Dodge Daytona. However, I found absolutely no indication of the drug in his system. There was zero chance of dangers from drug interactions between Accutane, MDMA and FH because it wasn't in Ashley's system at the time of the crash.

**Mary-Ellen:** Was it possible to tell whether he may have taken Accutane in the weeks or months before the accident?

**Dr. Todt:** It is my opinion that Ashley White had not been on the drug Accutane for months, perhaps a year, based upon what his parents shared with me.

**Mary-Ellen:** Is it possible that the two drugs interacted within Ashley's system in a toxic way? Could they have killed him, aside from their causing him to drive recklessly, crash and die?

**Dr. Todt:** In my opinion Ashley White was not killed by the drugs directly. Rather, he was probably suffering side effects from the drugs as he drove along the road after he left school on May 13. He was probably in a state of extreme disorientation at the time of the accident. He probably was going through wild mood swings; alternating between a detached euphoria from MDMA and the lows associated with MDMA's interaction with FH. Ashley probably had no idea how fast he was going while under the influence of these two drugs. But, let me caution you, just because both drugs were found in his system doesn't prove someone else criminally introduced them to Ashley's system.

**Mary-Ellen:** So what would you say was the direct cause of Ashley's death?

**Dr. Todt:** Ashley White died as a result of severe intracranial hemorrhage—bleeding inside the skull, in the brain [17]. This internal bleeding was severe and irreparable. This injury was caused by the telephone pole. During the accident, the pole caved in the passenger side roof, which, in turn, struck Ashley White in the head.

**Mary-Ellen:** What other injuries did you observe that were attributable to the car crash?

**Dr. Todt:** Ashley White had several broken bones and multiple skull fractures. His left forearm was broken in several places. This was probably caused by impact with the driver's side door. There were also multiple broken ribs on Ashley's left side, also caused by impacting the driver's side door.

Ashley was ejected from the vehicle as a result of the torque [18] generated by hitting the pole at an angle as the car was already up on two wheels—skidding. After being thrown from the Dodge Daytona, Ashley landed on a bush and a branch/stick punctured his left lung, causing it to completely collapse and fill with blood. He drowned in his own blood at the scene of the crash. There was nothing anyone could have done to save him.

**Mary-Ellen:** Did you find an injury to Ashley's head that could be attributed to his fall in class that day?

Was there a head injury that had resulted from Ashley striking his head on the heating/AC unit in class?

**Dr. Todt:** I found a relatively minor injury above the left eye. The injury was not caused by the auto accident. The shape of the bruise matched up with the edge of the heating/AC unit. The injury was on the forehead. It was bruised and raised. I can say with 100% confidence that this injury happened prior to the accident. This wound is consistent with what Ms. Lehrer and other students in her class saw when Ashley fell in class.

**Mary-Ellen:** Is there any chance that this contusion [19] to the head could have caused internal bleeding and ultimately concussion [20], disorientation [21] and bizarre behavior—leading to his reckless driving?

**Dr. Todt:** I do not believe that the fall that Ms. Lehrer and students describe would have been deadly in and of itself. But it's impossible to tell how bad the concussion was at that time, because of the severe nature of the injuries sustained later on—due to the crash. The crash certainly caused bleeding on the brain. That bleeding killed Ashley. The crash makes it impossible to differentiate with any degree of certainty.

On the other hand, it is certainly possible that Ashley had a severe concussion from the classroom fall. This concussion may very well explain his erratic behavior in school and may have been a contributing factor in the car crash later.

# Addendum to the Dr. Todt Interview

Since this interview is filled with terms that I myself was unfamiliar with, I am including explanations and definitions of the terms that most people reading this report will probably not know or be confused about. I've placed a number in brackets by the word so readers can easily reference them by going back and forth between the interview and this addendum.

## 1. Forensic Pathologist:

a medical doctor who has completed training in anatomical pathology and who has subsequently sub-specialized in forensic pathology. The requirements for becoming a "fully qualified" forensic pathologist varies from country to country. Some of the different requirements are discussed below.

They perform autopsies/postmortem examinations to determine the cause of death. The autopsy report contains an opinion about:

The pathologic process, injury, or disease that directly results in or initiates a series of events that lead to a person's death, such as a bullet wound to the head, a stab wound, manual or ligature strangulation, a heart attack resulting from disease, etc.), and

The "manner of death", the circumstances surrounding the cause of death, which include:

    Homicide
    Accidental
    Natural
    Suicide
    Undetermined

The autopsy also provides an opportunity for other issues raised by the death to be addressed, such as the collection of trace evidence or determining the identity of the deceased.

Examines and documents wounds and injuries, both at autopsy and occasionally in a clinical setting.

Collects and examines tissue specimens under the microscope (histology) in order to identify the presence or absence of natural disease and other microscopic findings such as asbestos bodies in the lungs or gunpowder particles around a gunshot wound.

Collects and interprets toxicological analyses on body tissues and fluids to determine the chemical cause of accidental overdoses or deliberate poisonings.

Source:
http://en.wikipedia.org/wiki/Forensic_pathology


## 2. **Coroner:**

A coroner is a government official who confirms and certifies the death of an individual. They may also conduct or order an investigation into the manner or cause of death, and investigate or confirm the identity of an unknown person who has been found dead. Responsibilities may include overseeing the investigation and certification of deaths. A coroner's office typically maintains death records of those who have died within the coroner's jurisdiction.

Source:
http://en.wikipedia.org/wiki/Coroner

## 3. **Autopsy:**

Also known as a "post-mortem"—is a highly specialized surgical procedure that consists of a thorough examination of a corpse to determine the cause and manner of death and to evaluate any disease or injury that may be present. It is usually performed by a specialized medical doctor called a pathologist.

Autopsies are performed for either legal or medical purposes. For example, a forensic autopsy is carried out when the cause of death may be a criminal matter.

Source:
http://en.wikipedia.org/wiki/Autopsy

## 4. **Methylenedioxymethamphetamine, (MDMA):**

This is a white, tan or brown powder, available primarily in tablet form.

Synonyms:
3,4-methylenedioxymethamphetamine;                ecstasy, ADAM, candy canes, disco biscuit, doves, E, eckie, essence, hug drug, love drug, M&M, rolls, white doves, X, XTC.

*Note: several of these terms come have come up in this case)*

Source:
MDMA is most commonly found in tablet forms of various colors, carrying distinctive markings on one side such as a dove, E, yin/yang symbol, Mitsubishi symbol, etc. MDMA is a Schedule I controlled substance.

Drug Class:
Mild CNS stimulant, empathogen, entactogen, mild hallucinogen and psychedelic, appetite suppressant.

Medical and Recreational Uses:
Originally patented as an appetite suppressant, there is now no legitimate medical use for it. It is used as at parties, raves (drug-enhanced dancing and socializing).

Potency, Purity and Dose:
MDMA is frequently taken with other recreational drugs such as ethanol, marijuana, cocaine, methamphetamine, nitrous oxide, and GHB.

How it is taken:
Primarily in pill form by mouth, although MDMA can be dissolved in liquids or injected, or crushed and snorted.

Effects:
MDMA has stimulant as well as psychedelic effects. MDMA is related in structure and effects to methamphetamine, however, it has significantly less CNS stimulant properties than methamphetamine. MDA, elicits more stereotypic behavior and is an even more potent neurotoxin than the parent drug. MDA destroys serotonin-producing neurons which play a direct role in regulating aggression, mood, sexual activity, sleep, and sensitivity to pain.

Psychological-Low to moderate doses (50-200 mg) produce mild intoxication, relaxation, euphoria, an excited calm or peace, feelings of well-being, increase in physical and emotional energy, increased sociability and closeness, heightened sensitivity, increased responsiveness to touch, changes in perception, and empathy. At higher doses, agitation, panic attacks, and illusory or hallucinatory experiences may occur.

Low to moderate doses (50-200 mg) produces mild visual disturbances (blurred or double vision, increased light sensitivity), dilated pupils, dry mouth, sweating, ataxia, muscle tension, and involuntary jaw clenching.

Other side effects include impairment of cognitive, perception, and mental associations, confusion, depression, sleep problems, other drug cravings, severe anxiety, and paranoia. People taking it may experience fatigue, uncoordinated gait, decreased fine motor skills, difficulty to maintain attention during complex tasks, preoccupation with small things, hyperthermia, tachycardia, hyperthermia, hyponatremia, convulsions, and catatonic stupor. Prolonged cognitive and behavioral effects may occur including poor memory recall, flashbacks, panic attacks, psychosis, and depersonalization due to neuron damage and decreased serotonin production as a result of long-term use.

Duration of Effects:
Following oral administration, effects onset in 20-30 minutes and desired effects may last only an hour or more, depending on dose. Other general effects last for approximately 2-3 hours. LSD is sometimes used in combination with MDMA to increase its duration of effects. Residual and unwanted effects are generally gone within 24 hours although confusion, depression and anxiety may last several weeks.

Tolerance, Dependence and Withdrawal Effect:

Drug stacking refers to the ingestion of single doses consecutively as effects begin to wane, similar to cocaine or methamphetamine binges. Such extensive or binge use usually occurs over weekends, and can result in exhaustion, apathy, depression, irritability, insomnia, and muscle tension early the next week. Tolerance does develop, however, the occurrence of physical and/or psychological dependence is unknown. Persistent neurological deficits may occur, including brain damage of various sorts.

Performance Effects:
MDMA can enhance impulsivity and make it difficult for a person to maintain attention during complex tasks. Studies have demonstrated changes in cognitive, perception and mental associations, instability, uncoordinated gait, and poor memory recall. Distortion of perception, thinking, and memory, impaired tracking ability, disorientation to time and place, and slow reactions are also known performance effects. Single oral doses of MDMA cause subjective excitability, anxiety, perceptual changes, and thought disorders 1-3 hours post dose.

For more information about the effects on drivers/driving, read the sourced, online article, below.

source:
http://www.nhtsa.gov/people/injury/research/job185 drugs/methylenedioxymethamphetamine.htm

## 5. Metabolism:

The amount of energy (calories) your body burns to maintain itself. Whether you are eating, drinking, sleeping, cleaning etc...your body is constantly burning calories to keep you going.  In this case the word applies to how quickly a person takes a drug into their system and how quickly it has an effect on them.

## 6. Black Market:

1. The illegal business of buying or selling goods or currency in violation of restrictions such as price controls or rationing.
2. A place where these illegal operations are carried on.

source:
http://www.thefreedictionary.com/black+market



## 7. Ingested/Ingestion:

The act of taking food and drink into the body by the mouth.

source:
http://medicaldictionary.thefreedictionary.com/ingesti
on



## 8. Fluoxetine Hydrochloride (aka, Prozac):

An oral antidepressant (drug) that acts by selectively preventing serotonin re-uptake. It is prescribed for major depressive disorder, obsessive-compulsive disorder, and bulemia nervosa.

Serious adverse effects include seizures, hemorrhage, tachycardia, bradycardia, myocardial infarction, and thrombophlebitis.

For the source and more information about side-effects,etc., go to:
http://medical-dictionary.thefreedictionary.com/fluoxetine+hydrochloride

## 9. **Antidepressant:**

Any of a class of drugs used to alleviate depression.

A medicine used to treat other conditions, on- or off-label, for conditions such as anxiety disorders, obsessive compulsive disorder, eating disorders, chronic pain, and some hormone-mediated disorders such as dysmenorrhea, and for snoring, migraines, attention-deficit hyperactivity disorder, (ADHD) substance abuse and occasionally even insomnia. Antidepressants are used either alone or combination with other medications.

Source:
http://www.thefreedictionary.com/antidepressant

## 10. **Insomnia:**

Typically called "sleeplessness," it is a sleep disorder in which there is an inability to fall asleep or to stay asleep as long as desired.

Insomnia is often practically defined as a positive response to either of two questions: "Do you experience difficulty sleeping?" or "Do you have difficulty falling or staying asleep?"

Insomnia is most often thought of as both a sign and a symptom that can accompany several sleep, medical, and psychiatric disorders characterized by a persistent difficulty falling asleep and/or staying asleep or sleep of poor quality. Insomnia is typically followed by functional impairment while awake. Insomnia can occur at any age, but it is particularly common in the elderly. Insomnia can be short term (up to three weeks) or long term (above 3–4 weeks), which can lead to memory problems, depression, irritability and an increased risk of heart disease and automobile related accidents.

Insomnia can be grouped into primary and secondary. Primary insomnia is a sleep disorder not attributable to a medical, psychiatric, or environmental cause. It is described as a complaint of prolonged sleep onset latency, disturbance of sleep maintenance, or the experience of non-refreshing sleep.

Source:
http://en.wikipedia.org/wiki/Insomnia

## 11. **Somnolence:**

Usually called "drowsiness," it is a state of near-sleep, a strong desire for sleep, or sleeping for unusually long periods (hypersomnia). It has two distinct meanings, referring both to the usual state preceding falling asleep, and the chronic condition referring to being in that state independent of a circadian rhythm. "Somnolence" is derived from the Latin "somnus" meaning "sleep."

Source:
http://en.wikipedia.org/wiki/Somnolence


## 12. **Anorexia:**

Anorexia nervosa is an eating disorder and, more importantly, a psychological disorder.

The cause of anorexia has not been definitively established, but self-esteem and body-image issues, societal pressures, and genetic factors likely each play a role.

Anorexia affects females far more often than males and is most common in adolescent females.

Anorexia tends to affect the middle and upper socioeconomic classes and Caucasians more often than less advantaged classes and ethnic minorities in the United States.

The disorder affects about 1% of adolescent girls and about 0.3% of males in the U.S.

People with anorexia tend to show compulsive behaviors, may become obsessed with food, and often show behaviors consistent with other addictions in their efforts to overly control their food intake and weight.

Men with anorexia are more likely to also have other psychological problems; affected women tend to be more perfectionist-types and hyper-critical of their bodies.

Children and adolescents with anorexia are at risk for a slowing of their growth and development.

The extreme dieting and weight loss of anorexia can lead to a potentially fatal degree of malnutrition.

Other possible complications of anorexia include heart-rhythm disturbances, digestive abnormalities, bone density loss, anemia, and hormonal and electrolyte imbalances.

Source:
http://www.medicinenet.com/anorexia_nervosa/article.htm

## 13. **Asthenia:**

Lack of energy and strength. Loss of strength. Myasthenia refers to a loss of muscle strength, as in myasthenia gravis.

Asthenia is from the Greek asthenes, from a- (without) + sthenos (strength).

Source:
http://www.medterms.com/script/main/art.asp?articlekey=32122

## 14. **Tremors:**

Tremors are an unintentional, rhythmic muscle movement involving to-and-fro movements of one or more parts of the body. It is the most common of all involuntary movements and can affect the hands, arms, head, face, voice, trunk, and legs. Most tremors occur in the hands. In some people, tremor is a symptom of a neurological disorder or appears as a side effect of certain drugs. The most common form of tremor, however, occurs in otherwise largely healthy people. Although tremor is not life-threatening, it can be embarrassing to some people and make it harder to perform daily tasks.

What causes tremors?

Tremors are generally caused by problems in parts of the brain that control muscles throughout the body or in particular areas, such as the hands. Neurological disorders or conditions that can produce tremor include multiple sclerosis, stroke, traumatic brain injury, and neurodegenerative diseases that damage or destroy parts of the brainstem or the cerebellum. Other causes include the use of some drugs (such as amphetamines, corticosteroids, and drugs used for certain psychiatric disorders), alcohol abuse or withdrawal, mercury poisoning, overactive thyroid, or liver failure. Some forms of tremor are inherited and run in families, while others have no known cause.

What are the characteristics of tremor?

Characteristics may include a rhythmic shaking in the hands, arms, head, legs, or trunk; shaky voice; difficulty writing or drawing; or problems holding and controlling utensils, such as a fork. Some tremors may be triggered by or become exaggerated during times of stress or strong emotion, when the individual is physically exhausted, or during certain postures or movements.

Tremor may occur at any age but is most common in middle-aged and older persons. It may be occasional, temporary, or occur intermittently. Tremor affects men and women equally.

A useful way to understand and describe tremors is to define them according to the following types. Resting tremor occurs when the muscle is relaxed, such as when the hands are lying on the lap or hanging next to the trunk while standing or walking. It may be seen as a shaking of the limb, even when the person is at rest. Often, the tremor affects only the hand or fingers. This type of tremor is often seen in patients with Parkinson's disease. An action tremor occurs during any type of movement of an affected body part. There are several sub classifications of action tremor. Postural tremor occurs when the person maintains a position against gravity, such as holding the arms outstretched. Kinetic tremor appears during movement of a body part, such as moving the wrists up and down, while intention tremor is present during a purposeful movement toward a target, such as touching a finger to one's nose during a medical exam. Task-specific tremor appears when performing highly skilled, goal-oriented tasks such as handwriting or speaking. Isometric tremor occurs during a voluntary muscle contraction that is not accompanied by any movement.

Source:
http://www.medicinenet.com/tremor/article.htm


## 15. **EMT:**

What They Do-

Emergency medical technicians (EMTs) and paramedics care for the sick or injured in emergency medical settings. People's lives often depend on their quick reaction and competent care. EMTs and paramedics respond to emergency calls, performing medical services and transporting patients to medical facilities.

Emergency medical technicians (EMTs) and paramedics work both indoors and outdoors, in all types of weather. Their work is physically strenuous and can be stressful, sometimes involving life-or-death situations and patients who are suffering.

How to Become an EMT or Paramedic

All EMTs and paramedics must complete a formal training program. All states require EMTs and paramedics to be licensed; requirements vary by state.

Source:
http://www.bls.gov/ooh/healthcare/emts-and-paramedics.htm

## 16. Accutane:

Is a form of vitamin A. It reduces the amount of oil released by oil glands in your skin, and helps your skin renew itself more quickly.

Accutane is used to treat severe nodular acne. It is usually given after other acne medicines or antibiotics have been tried without successful treatment of symptoms.

Accutane is available only under a special program called iPLEDGE. The user must be registered in the program and sign documents stating that they understand the dangers of this medication.

Source:
http://www.drugs.com/accutane.html

## 17. Intracranial Hemorrhage:

ICH, for short, is bleeding within the skull.  ICH occurs when a blood vessel within the skull is ruptured or leaks. It can result from a head injury or non-traumatic causes, like a stroke.

Source:
http://en.wikipedia.org/wiki/Intracranial_hemorrhage

## 18. Torque:

Torque is a force that tends to rotate or turn something. For example, you generate a torque any time you apply a force using a wrench. Tightening the lug nuts on your wheels is another good example. When you use a wrench, you apply a force to the handle. This force creates a torque on the lug nut, which tends to turn the lug nut.

This can apply to the movement of the body when acted upon by an outside force.

Source:
http://auto.howstuffworks.com/auto-parts/towing/towing-capacity/information/fpte4.htm

## 19. **Contusion:**

Usually called a bruise, "contusion" is the proper medical term.  It is a type of bleeding of tissue in which capillaries are damaged by trauma, allowing blood to seep, and bleed into the surrounding tissues. Not blanching on pressure, bruises can involve capillaries at the level of skin, subcutaneous tissue, muscle, or bone.

Source:
http://en.wikipedia.org/wiki/Bruise

## 20. **Concussion:**

The most common and least serious type of trauma to the brain. The word comes from the Latin "concutere" which means "to shake violently."

A concussion is most often caused by a sudden direct blow or bump to the head.

The brain is made of soft tissue. It's cushioned by spinal fluid and encased in the protective shell of the skull. When you sustain a concussion, the impact can jolt your brain. Sometimes, it literally causes it to move around in your head. Traumatic brain injuries can cause bruising, damage to the blood vessels, and injury to the nerves.

The result is that the brain doesn't function normally. If you've suffered a concussion, your vision may be disturbed, you may lose equilibrium, or you may become unconscious. In short, the brain is confused.

Source:
http://www.webmd.com/brain/concussion-traumatic-brain-injury-symptoms-causes-treatments


## 21. **Disorientation:**

A mental condition in which the senses of time, direction, and recognition of people and places become difficult to distinguish.

Source:
Isaac M., Janca A., Sartious N., 1994.ICD-10 Symptom Glossary For Mental Disorders,10th ed. WHO.

# Frank Thomas

The following is the transcript of my interview with
Mr. Frank Thomas, conducted in Room 104 at
Franklin High School, Jedesdorf, PA.

Date: June 25, 2011
Time: 1:40-2:23 PM
Witness: Mr. Roger D. Flory (Teacher).


**Mary-Ellen:** I know this is a rough thing for you to
re-live. I really appreciate that you've consented to this
interview. Tell me about the fatal accident you
witnessed on Monday, May 13.

**Mr. Thomas:** It was after work. I go jogging every
day after work. I was jogging along the Route 429
when a white Dodge Daytona flew by at a high rate of
speed. It was out of control. As it crested the hill by
Stubbville Road the driver lost it. The car skidded off
the road to the left, across the double line and hit a
telephone pole. The car spun around violently,
breaking the telephone pole in two. Dust and
splintering wood flew every which way. I saw the
driver thrown from the vehicle as the door opened
after hitting the telephone pole.

After the dust settled and I got over the initial
disbelief that I had just seen an accident, I ran over to
find a teenage boy laying face up at the bottom of a
nearby ditch. The car had come to rest, upside down.
I can still remember the weird sounds the car made. It
hissed and the wheels were still spinning slowly. I

could smell gas and the smell of rubber from the skid. The car had skidded quite a distance.

**Mary-Ellen:** You're shaking. Take a minute to compose yourself. Have a sip of water.

After all this time, over a year later, you're still upset. It must have been horrible, something you'll never forget. I'm Sorry.

**Mr. Thomas:** I will never forget it, that's for sure. I wanted to save the boys life, but I could do *nothing*. He died in front of me before the ambulance arrived.

**Mary-Ellen:** Do you remember when, exactly, he died?

**Mr. Thomas:** Ashley White died around 4:18. I know this because I remember looking at my watch as the ambulance pulled up. It was 4:21.

**Mary-Ellen:** Did you try to move Ashley?

**Mr. Thomas:** No, the dispatcher told me not to move him. I had called 9-1-1 right away, even before I found him in the ditch.

**Mary-Ellen:** It sounds like you had trouble locating him at first.

**Mr. Thomas:** Yes. I couldn't find the driver. It took about a minute before I heard a faint wheezing and gurgling sound. The sound was coming from the bottom of a drainage ditch, about fifteen feet from the upside down car.

**Mary-Ellen:** Was he conscious when you found him?

**Mr. Thomas:** He was. I'll never forget the look of fear in his eyes. He clearly knew he was dying. I pleaded with the dispatcher to tell me what to do after describing his injuries to her.

**Mary-Ellen:** What did she say you should do?

**Mr. Thomas:** She told me to "stay put" and to "try to keep Ashley awake". She told me to "try to talk with him in a comforting way".

**Mary-Ellen:** What did you say or do?

**Mr. Thomas:** I held his free hand. His other hand was bent underneath his torso. He was in pain. I held his hand and told him that the ambulance would be coming soon.

**Mary-Ellen:** Could he respond to you?

**Mr. Thomas:** I wasn't sure if he was talking or not at first. He was trying to talk. He made the strangest rattling sound as he breathed. Then he coughed and spit out blood. After he cleared his throat, he tried to pull me down to his face. He was trying to talk but he could barely get the words out.

**Mary-Ellen:** What did he say?

**Mr. Thomas:** He took one final breath as if to gather his remaining strength, locked onto my eyes and said, "Tell M&M...I'm sorry. Tell my parents...and Paisley...I love them..."

**Marty Fine did not consent to an interview.**

# Final Thoughts

I hope someone, somewhere, will pick up this book and pursue this case in a court of criminal law. I've done everything I can think of to get to the bottom of this case, to re-ignite interest in it, to get the District Attorney's Office to re-open an investigation, to provoke them into bringing the evidence before a grand jury.

It hasn't worked.

So, now it's up to you. I bring this to you as an unfinished work. It's up to you to write the last chapter, to conduct the final interview, to connect the dots that I may have missed, and to bring justice to Ashley White.

The ball is in your court. I challenge you to write the ending to this story, and if not to this one, another one by the same theme. Same theme? Yes. Write your own and become part of my quest to end the scourge of insidious bullying, the sort of bullying that you know goes on every day, all across this nation. It's not the obvious bullies who are the real danger, and everyone reading this knows it.

As I mentioned at the beginning, the Franklin High School Board of Education requires a graduation project from all students. This work represents many more than the 60 hours of community service necessary to fulfill that mandate. In support of this fact

I have kept a log.  More than 200 hours were spent putting together this project.

Will any members of the Franklin School Board even take the time to read this?

I don't know. I hope so.

I'd love to hear from you, to read and listen to your theories and insights about this case.  I'd love to hear from people who find evidence and testimony that I've overlooked.

You are my citizen grand jury.


**Sincerely Yours,**


*Mary-Ellen Gerhard*

Made in the USA
Monee, IL
07 July 2026

56551150R00144